NICHOLAS FERRANTE

DEAR JOHN

NIXCOMIX
PUBLISHING

DEAR JOHN

Published by NixComix Publishing
nixcomix.com

ISBN (print): 979-8-9870103-9-6
ISBN (e-book): 979-8-9870103-8-9

An application to register this book for cataloguing has been submitted to the Library of Congress.
First Edition: January 2024

Cover design by Spirit's Paintbrush
Editing by Sean Leonard
Interior art by Yelenhol

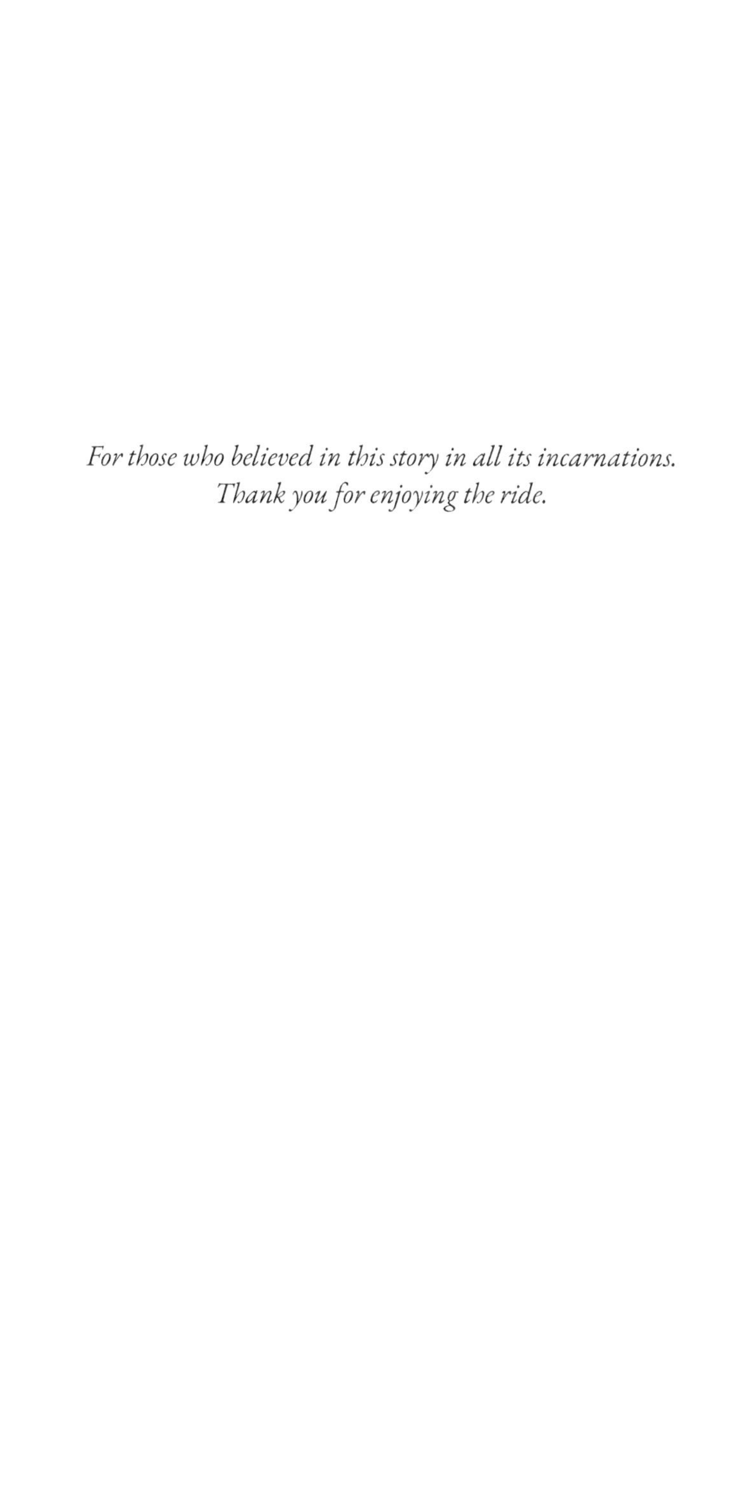

For those who believed in this story in all its incarnations.
Thank you for enjoying the ride.

Surprise

Blood fills his mouth, that unmistakable metallic tang. His limbs electrify back to life with a vicious, needling ache that takes over all other sensation. Everything around him is a blank, black void of no one, nowhere, and nothing.

He can't see.

Why can't he see?

His awareness gradually comes back online, and a dull pain descends as he awakens. His mouth is cracked, dry and… something else.

Something is wrong.

A great many things are *wrong*.

Someone nearby is crying, hoarse, wet, and heavy. Sniveling and snotty. He doesn't know if it's male or female. The whining strands of it are too bleating to tell the difference. All he knows is that it's a stranger; he's been alone far too long for it to be anything else.

A strangled sound lets out, followed by a heavy *thud*, and the high-pitched panting of panic. Screams come, muffled and dimmed, as if from behind a heavy pillow, like a teenager throwing its rage into their bedding, not wanting anyone to hear. A foreign something cranks, dragging the screaming voice closer. Closer. Louder. Loudest. The skitter of dust and dirt echoes as those muted hollers scrape past him and into the void beyond. They wane into the distance until they've faded away, leaving only silence and the sound of his own heartbeat.

Senses registering one by one, his body ramps up to call out its agony in different notes. His nerve endings sizzle and clamor for attention as he flexes the fingers stuck painfully behind his back, and begs himself to *WakeUpWake-UpWakeUp*.

A clack of steps breaks the quiet into pieces. Boots. Heavy ones. Heel, toe, heel, toe, coming closer.

Someone stands before him now. The bright red capillaries behind his closed eyelids dim to a deep burgundy as the newcomer casts a shadow on his face. Their heat rolls over him as he struggles to process the simplest of thoughts.

Is he shaking?

Is it cold?

Crisp nails rake their way through his hair, not unkindly. Almost affectionately. A cooing whisper fills his ears, "Good boy, John."

And his bladder lets go.

John's head jerks back and forth as he tries to blink, but his eyes won't open. The world upsy-daisies as he tries to wrench his body from whatever he's sitting on, his weight shifting as he begins to freefall. Instinct alone makes him curl his head forward, saving his skull as his back hits a cold surface with a jarring *thwack*. His head ricochets, and he sees stars through his blind eyes when it bashes. Whatever was beneath him has broken apart, letting him uncurl, and he stretches through his body's multiplying protests.

Where am I? His mind swirls those words around. Each

time they pound harder, more real and more dangerous. *Where the fuck am I?*

Those boots walk away. Far. Farther. Inaudible. Then closer once more. John's ankles scrape against...rope? He struggles for a heated moment but freezes when something metallic drags on the floor. Slow. One pull at a time. A sort of *shiiiiiink, shiiiiiiiinnnnnnnk.*

Cold metal is hooked between his feet and into his bindings. When he drops his jaw to scream, he tastes fresh blood, something ripping his flesh as his lips remain sealed.

Just like his eyes.

The secret someone clucks their tongue and shushes him as if John were a spooked animal. Somehow that makes everything worse. His breath comes quickly in snot-riddled sucks, and his head swims with the heady oxygen. If he keeps this up, he's going to faint.

Those boots step away. Only moments pass before that vicious crank cries out again, making John's muscles lock. Like the stranger, he cascades over the floor, his back turning to fire.

Concrete. He's on *concrete.*

Flesh grates as he slides forward in a painful rush, adrenaline howling through his body. His sealed eyes burn with the salt sting of tears, and there's a mechanical whir as he drags. It barely registers. His world is a narrowed pinprick of pain.

The unexpected *thump-thump* of his body against metal indicates he's crossed some kind of threshold. He can hear the screaming stranger again, sobbing this time, low and smothered. *Male,* John decides airily, on the verge of delirium. He runs his raspy tongue over the inside of his lips and feels... threads. Stitches.

His stomach flip-flops.

His mouth has been sewn shut.

It's then that his deformed bellows match that of the

screaming stranger. His body makes one last ripping slide before he slams into the man who immediately begins squirming. The stranger reeks of piss, blood, and the acrid tang of sweat. It's this scent more than anything else that makes John realize the nightmare is real.

His legs are tugged around and released from the metal crank they were hooked to. They land heavily onto the other man, who tries to scrabble away without much luck. They must be outside. Crickets sing a death march in the cool, stinging night air, and John's hyper-aware brain hears every stroke of their symphony. The chill itself hurts. His fever must be coming back, joining his choir of other pains.

A diesel motor kicks on with a sputtering grumble. The smell reminds him of gas stations, unfriendly attendants, and packets of sickly-sweet gum lacing the counter tops in silver foil packets. Of his father fixing junky cars, waiting for the engine to finally turn over as he tweaked the key on repeat. The scent is both nostalgic and unmistakable. He's in the back of a truck. A big one. Underneath the other stinks is the scent of cut grass, out of place in the human stench around him.

What the fuck is happening? The raging sentiment beats in time with his heart.

The truck starts to move beneath them, a wobbling bumpiness, like driving on uneven ground. The screaming stranger is all pushing feet and elbows, trying to buck John off, but there's nowhere to go. John's chin gets hammered with a heel, knocking more stars into his blinded vision, and it's too much. He starts to quake, tense muscles jittering under the bulk of the male who's wriggled his way above him.

Dry gears grind to a squealing halt, but there is no open-shut door sound, only a mechanical whir, and the platform beneath them shifts into a growing tilt. Steep. Steeper. Steepest. The screaming stranger keens as they start to slide again, this time down the harsh angle of the metallic slab. Down to where? Nowhere good.

John wedges his raw back and his feet against opposite sides of the truck bed, trying to pin himself in place as the other man's body scrapes down the length of the platform. For a moment, the only sound is the hiss of the stranger's body-slide, but then there's a sharp squawk before a harsh *thwump* echoes from somewhere below.

I don't wanna go there. Please, for the love of God, don't make me go there.

The stranger howls now, and John's muscles are straining, trembling, fading, until he, too, is taken on a vicious ride and finds himself airborne.

It lasts forever. It's split seconds. The stranger's shrieks are ear-splitting...until John lands.

A sickening *crack* jars every inch of him, and silence falls, leaving only the pounding in his head and the now-distant crickets. John's body came down on top of the screaming stranger, and his noisy companion no longer makes a sound. No weeping. No writhing. No whimpers.

No breathing.

The screaming stranger is dead.

And John blacks out.

———

Heat.

Whispers.

Unconsciousness.

———

Cold biting his flesh with jagged teeth.
    Jabs. Finger pokes.
        Whispers like feathers in the air.
        Nothingness.

———

Chills and trembling.

His body hates him. John can feel its angry scolds with his fevered cheeks.

Water then. Cool. John finds he can part his lips, and his body opens like a flower to receive every drop. He tries to speak but can't. His throat is swollen and closed in on itself, its insides rubbing roughly with every swallow.

Hands are on him—pressing, prodding—and a disembodied voice sighs. "...fever. If we don't do something, he'll probably die anyway."

"Then don't waste the water," a thick voice mutters.

"Maybe she'll give us meds?" the first voice tries.

"Yeah. Good luck with that."

John coughs a single wet exhale...and blacks out once more.

———

Water again. The taste of bubblegum liquid. Sticky, delicious, cold, and somehow wrong in the present circumstance. John tries to open his eyes, but they're still anchored shut. His eyebrows knit as he winces.

Words echo, soft and soothing. "Careful, not yet. We fixed your mouth but, well..."

Somewhere in his mind, John knows that sentence should raise alarm, it's the sort of thing that ought to, but he's too sick and too tired to do anything but accept. *Mouth fixed. Eyes not. Check.* He floats above, registering his body in only the most detached of ways.

A strip of meat is put between his lips, salty—which stings—but his body wants it, so he accepts. It comes in little, tiny bits he doesn't even have to chew before swallowing.

More water, and this time he's able to take a couple mouthfuls.

His hands are in front of him now instead of behind, given some slack but still bound with ties that bite into the skin at his wrists. He tests his arms, slowly flexing and feeling their stiffness, the aching sensitivity from fever, and the extent of the bruising and scraped skin. Something tears open, and he hisses in a sharp breath of pain before barking out a series of rattling, phlegmy coughs that last far too long. His head is a pounding mess, and a slam of dizziness makes the blackness undulate beneath him like waves. Swirling like a tornado in a beaker, his stomach gives a good old *Fuck you,* and threatens to let go.

"Where...?" It's no more than a choked whisper.

Another voice lets out a harsh, sarcastic laugh. "Never mind. This is stupid."

The first voice comes back again. It's lower in volume but ice cold in tone. "No. We agreed. For once, we both agreed."

"Yeah? Well, we're both stupid."

The soft-voiced one murmurs, "This'll work...it has to." Dry hands begin to hold John's face and urge more water into him. Lowering a dark octave, the voice adds, "And if he can't do it, we'll take care of him your way."

John's mind begins to click like clockwork. The reality of the situation comes into picture-perfect focus.

Wherever he is, he is not safe.

————

Dampness trickles, uncomfortable and undoubtedly making John's skin crinkle like he's been in a bathtub for hours too long. He hears the light rain make a shushing sound, and he can feel droplets hitting his belly, hips, and legs in tiny spatters. The past few times he's woken up, he's found his admittedly flat backside lying over some sort of metal grate. He may or may not be naked. It's hard to tell.

The pattern of bars crisscrossing beneath him must be this place's version of a piddle pad. As the day goes on, his pride takes a backhanded clobber every time he tilts to the side to void his bladder, but the lashes around his ankles and wrists—not to mention the complete and utter blindness he finds himself in—make it hard to do much else. His eyes are swollen and hurt, but he refuses to touch them. He's afraid of what he'll find.

He's awake for hours at a time now. Today seems to be a whole day's worth. His fever is gone, but that deep ache remains, especially in his throat, tethered limbs, and shoulder blades. The concrete that tore stripes into him leaves a throb, but not a sting. Whatever damage it did is likely a mess of scabs. Probably ones that are sloughing off in the damp.

What a pleasant thought, he snarks to himself.

Sometimes it's completely silent when he's awake. Sometimes the grate is bathed in the sun, warming his hips and searing him a bit when he rolls. John's mind tries to grasp how many days he's been down here, fed and watered by strangers. And, oh, those strangers.

One is his nursemaid, pumping him full of beef jerky and liquid meds. *Amoxicillin,* his mind provides. The stuff kids get that tastes like bubblegum. He'd loved that stuff. Would fake being sick just to get some. Wanted it even when he was a teenager. His sixteen-year-old self would be jealous. Or not, considering.

The other voice, the harsh voice, doesn't talk unless he thinks John is sleeping, and when John hears that one, it always borders on angry. More than once, it's threatened to let John die or kill him outright. John has to struggle to keep from shuddering, crying out, or pissing himself when he hears the angry one come too close, his gritty footsteps and slight limp like an audible fingerprint.

John gathers his strength hour by hour, tracking the brightness that lights up his eyelids as the sun passes over him...wherever he is. Not too hot, not too cold, dank, dirt, and stone may as well be all that exists.

He pretends to be as weak as possible when it's feeding time. Eventually, his moratorium will end, and he wants to have the element of surprise, if not the upper hand, when whatever happens finally happens. His imagination centers on fights he's seen on TV, the lashing choreography of it, and tries to puzzle-piece together some semblance of what he could do if push came to shove. How he could bob and weave. Head-bash and bite. Truth be told, without his eyesight, he'd need some superhero hearing to pull off that miracle. He holds out no hope.

After a while, boredom prods him to finally risk sitting up, or trying to at any rate. It doesn't work. He gives up quickly with a grunt and hates himself for a few minutes, embarrassed of all things. It's one of those unnerving silent times, but he never really knows if he's alone or not. Who's out there watching him fail?

John's voice sounds strange and raw with disuse, his throat still sore. "H-hello? Is anyone there?" It echoes a little, like he's in a cavern. Or a catacomb.

Something shifts. Moves closer. John clenches his abs with a grunt, managing to get upright this time, but his head swims with a dangerous wave of dizziness. His wrists are still bound in front, putting him at a disadvantage, so he tightens, jaw to ankles, as he prepares to struggle. He will if he has to. The pitter-patter of raindrops soaks the grease of his unwashed hair as this moment of tension draws back like a bowstring.

"Are you dangerous?" asks the kinder voice. A ludicrous question, really.

Huffing out something like disbelief, John tries to pull from his bag of charming. "Only to myself." His smirk is self-deprecating and well-practiced. There's only one problem. He can't tell if his joke lands or not. Lost in the darkness, John's disadvantages multiply.

Clearing his throat, he tucks his sarcasm away, thinking of those hostage shows on TV.

Humanize yourself. You have to make them see that you're more than a body. You're a person. You're like them.

He tells the voice, "I'm not dangerous, I swear. I'm just a regular guy." Which he doesn't feel is entirely true. "I have no idea where I am. I'm scared and hurt, and I just want to go home." To what, he's not sure.

"We're all *scared,* and *hurt,* and *want to go home,*" the meaner voice hisses, making John wince.

Swallowing, he adds gently, "My name is John. What's yours?"

The angry voice speaks from all-too-close behind him. "Names don't matter down here."

"Will you shut up," Kind-voice says, exasperated more than anything else. John's sure he hears the other man growl.

"Look at him," Angry-voice intones with feigned sweetness. John can feel his nasty breath on the back of his neck. "Your little pet is sitting up all on his own. It's only a matter of time before it's too late." The man paces around John in a predatory circle, the padding of his feet too loud in this quiet place. "There isn't enough food, enough water, and she's gone for two more days."

Kind-voice cuts in, "Then we make this work for two more days."

"Are you," John asks, sounding purposefully meek, "are you keeping me here, or are you like me?"

"I am not like you!" Angry-voice yells, and John curls sharply in on himself.

With a sigh, Kind-voice ignores the outburst and says, "We're just like you. She put us down here. We've been down here a long ti—"

There is a scuffle then. John hides his face between his knees as sounds ricochet around him. In the damp, there is a throbbing echo of skin slapping skin, grunts, shoving, and dirt being skid on, kicking up rough dustings onto John's feet. Words are being muttered by the others, but John is too focused on his internal chant to hear them clearly. Childish words roll around in his mind. *If I hide, they won't see me. If I hide, they won't see me,* just like he used to think when there were monsters under his bed.

Finally, there is a hard *oof* and something thumps.

"You wanna die down here?"

John flinches...until he realizes that the words weren't directed at him.

"Because that's exactly what's going to happen. Look at us!"

John can't breathe fast enough. His lungs heave and pull, tears pooling behind his sealed eyes.

That voice, that once-kind-voice, shouts in his direction, "What year is it?"

John quakes and tells him on repeat like they're the only words he knows.

The volume in this place—this *down here*—drops, and Kind-voice quiets again. There's one more grunt and shove. "Three years," the man says in terrible awe. "We've been down here three *FUCKING YEARS!*" There is another shove. More slapping. More than a few yelps of pain and sharp intakes of breath until John's knees are downright knocking.

"Please stop," he begs. "Please, please, please."

I used to be so strong, John thinks. *Now look at me.* He thought he was on his way to rock bottom before, but now he's passed through the rickety floorboards he once imagined into an unknown, endless chasm.

Rough hands grab him, shoving him onto his back again, and he cries out in pathetic surprise when his shoulder blades reopen on the rough ground. His legs are hiked up and something cold is slipped between his ankles, making him squeal and buck.

"Stop," Angry-voice says. "If you kick me, I'll kill you."

And John doesn't think he's lying. Taking hitching breaths, he holds still and counts down, only just managing to hold his spiking anxiety at bay. He *will not* have another panic attack. Not here. Not now. He's not supposed to be an anxious man anymore. He's a confident one. One others look up to. But here in this place he's been reduced to something small.

With a quick wrench, the ropes around his ankles loosen. It makes him keep all the more still and hold his breath until it burns inside. Angry-voice pants as John's legs tug back and forth slightly. A rough sawing through the material causes little twangs until he's loose and looser and *free.*

With a soft sob, he holds out his wrists, praying for the same, but they're slapped away.

"Level one trust," Angry-voice states. *"One.* I don't have more of this,"—he wiggles the crippling rope still around John's wrists—"so I can't re-tie you. That means, if you give me trouble, I'll hamstring you instead. Yes?"

John clamps his lips together as his head jerks up and down.

"Good."

The rest of the day goes by in elongated silence until the red of the sun slips past John's eyelids. He curls into fetal position, knees to his chest, trying to protect anything that might be vital as he waits for the next phase of this horror show.

———

Too much time passes like that. Salted meat. Water. Pink meds. Silence. Tense, palpable, terrifying silence. John wants a drink. Some nice hard liquor to stave off his aches—body, mind, and soul. A heavy weight of loneliness grips him without the reprieve that comes with his usual distractions. No work. No phone. No women. No vices. So, he writes scripts in his head. It's been a while. He makes himself the star once more, remembering all the good advice he's given to others and applying that trash to himself. *You can do anything you set your mind to. Do it until you do it right.* He also tries desperately to understand why he's still alive, and on day two of complete lucidness, it clicks.

Scuffing his stubble over his shoulder, itchy as fuck, he feels the tone of his muscles. When Kind-voice feeds him, his hands are bony. Thin. He stinks of body odor and sick. If they've been...*down here*...for three years, they must be weak. Malnourished, maybe. Human husks, for all he knows. If they're sitting in this hellhole with him, he's guessing they're long overdue for an escape plan, and he might be it. Maybe his strength matters. Maybe his newness matters. They're working hard enough to keep him alive, anyway. Well, one of them is.

Still, he bides his time and works on the puzzle of now. When he asks who they are, he gets guarded answers. Angry-voice just repeats "Names don't matter" with varying levels of threat in his tone. John stops asking.

And on what he can only guess is day three, he finally meets *her*.

Again.

———

She laughs out loud, startling John from an uncomfortable, nightmare-filled slumber. The feminine sound of her is oddly enchanting, as if she was romping around some candy-coated fairground instead of cornering three trapped men. The tinkling bell of her giggle strikes John as oddly familiar. Sickeningly so. It seems to come from directly above, and his follicles tighten, hairs standing on end as little electric pulses twitch him in terrified flinches. Someone has officially grabbed his life's remote and pressed play.

"He's milking it, you know," she says in singsong, and John can hear the others shuffle at her words. "If he's not up an at 'em by now, he's fooling you. That one's full of tricks, believe me."

John blindly tries to make himself small.

Her voice drops an octave, making her sound like some

blasé doctor reading from a chart. "It was just a concussion. And a fever, but I already knew he was sick when I brought him in. I think he even gave it to me a little, the bastard." She sniffles. "Either way, meds and meat make happy men, right? So he should be fine and dandy by now. Unless he's faking it, of course." She takes on a sly tone. "He's probably just trying to get more than his fair share."

She says it as if that wasn't a dangerous statement. Her voice is affectionate when she calls down the word "Stupid" as if it was a term of endearment.

With a grunt, what must be the angry one lunges toward John, and he tries to backpedal away from the sound. He can't stand fast enough and finds his hair yanked back, a sharp something pressing against his throat.

The woman above *tsk*s. "I thought you wanted a friend. I gave him to you to play with. You'd get rid of my present so easily?" It's said with that lilt of amusement. "You left him basically handcuffed and blinded. Why would he trust you at level two?"

"Level two," the man behind John repeats in a whisper, the implement of destruction trembling against his skin. A moment passes before there is another sharp yank, John crying out as his neck is pulled backward at a severe angle. Angry-voice growls at him. "If you don't hold still, things are going to go sideways very fast."

John feels flicks of pain on his eyelids, the sharp something picking and plucking and pulling, making his eyes water. Peering through his lashes, nearly a foreign concept at this point, he can see black, jail bar-esque lines over his field of vision.

With a hard, rough rip, the last of his bindings are sheared off with that same makeshift blade, and John's wrists are freed. He's shoved to the ground, mewling, as he pulls tiny threads from his eyelids with trembling hands. His stomach threatens to empty its nothingness on the ground as he loses count of how many stitches held him in the darkness all this time.

When he finally looks up, the light is like staring directly into the sun. Two human wraiths hover over him, backlit in chiaroscuro as a halo of bright white frames them like dying angels.

Kind-voice nods his head slightly. "Welcome to the Fishbowl."

THE PAST -
Interlude Eight

The wooden bar top glows under the neon lights advertising all the beers no one wants to drink. Who the hell needs micro-brewed craft beer anyway? A Bud is a Bud is a Bud. Or in John's case, a whiskey is a whiskey is a whiskey.

He snuffles back. He has strep; he can tell. His body aches with that tell-tale "I need antibiotics" refrain, but the alcohol has tamped that down to a dull roar. Damned if he'll see a doctor. He hates doctors.

Catching him by surprise, a sharp red fingernail caresses the space where John's wedding ring should be. No matter how long it's been off, it's like a permanent indent in his body, and the foreign touch on his second biggest failure startles him out of his drifting buzz. A body is warm beside him —too close, too intimate—and that's alright with him. He doesn't say anything for a minute and just watches the tender stroke of a stranger with sexy red promises painted on her fingertips.

After he doesn't buck her off, she sits next to him. Again, perfectly too close. John doesn't look to see if she's pretty. It doesn't matter one way or the other; he's not picky, so long as she's warm.

"Buy me a drink," she says. Not a question, an assumption. Local bar, though. John has few rules, but one of them is that he doesn't inspire any second-tryst illusions. One night only, no matter what. He has enough messiness in his life.

He sniffles and clears his sore throat. "You from around here?" he asks, still not bothering to look at her face.

She giggles. It's a bright, happy little thing. "God, no. Just here on business. Too cold for me." She makes a cute little *brrr* shiver he can see out of the corner of his eye.

"I've been told I make a good blanket," he says. A smile blooms on his face as he falls into familiar platitudes, so rote he doesn't even have to think about them. "If you stay close like this, I can keep you from catching a chill." *And probably get you sick while I'm at it.*

Whatever she says next doesn't matter. He can't really focus on her words right now anyway. It's the tone of her voice that makes all the difference, and that silky sound remains interested, from what he can tell.

She blurs a bit as he finally looks at her. He feels nice and fuzzy-brained at this point, his focus narrowing in on her lips as she blathers. Her smile is something else. Pretty teeth, pretty mouth. That mouth says it knows what it's doing. He can't help but hope her lipstick's not that long-lasting crap. That stuff doesn't leave its sweet little puckers on him the way it should. He likes it when they leave marks, letting him wake up and see their smooches in the mirror in the morning. He gives them hickeys and fingerprint-shaped bruises on their hips, and they leave him with something that belongs at the bottom of love letters.

It's her lips and those sexy red nails that keep dragging along his non-wedding ring that make him want her. She's probably getting off on the thought of picking up someone looking to cheat. Some women are into that. Hell, he's into it too. A sort of nihilistic, "Let's ruin our lives together" kind of thing.

Rubbing at the dent that encircles his skin, she asks, "Is that only for tonight?"

He looks at it wistfully. "It's for forever."

"Liar," she chides, but it's laced with something soft and amused.

He smiles at her, taking another sip from his drink, soothing his raw throat. The deep amber doesn't even burn anymore. "You have a nice voice." Bold, probably too bold, he murmurs, "I can't wait to hear it get husky."

She hums some sort of agreement, stepping her fingers up his arm to his shoulder and making his body pay attention. "And you think you'll get the privilege?"

For better or for worse, "I usually do."

He scolds himself for being too cocky, going too fast. He has half a mind to blame it on the booze and apologize, but her giggles go from a tinkling bell to a hearty belly laugh, making him laugh along too.

"Now that I can believe." She curls her fingers into little claws and runs them down his forearm, leaving goosebumps in their wake. Seems she likes going too fast. Good for her.

Her voice drops to a whisper. "Wanna get out of h—"

"Absolutely. Yes, and yes. And please," he says, his next charming flash of teeth bordering on wolfish. He tosses cash down on the bar...though, did he actually buy her a drink? He can't remember.

When they stumble outside, he is, by far, the more stumbly of the two, but the cold air brings his senses back toward baseline. Eyeing her, she's pretty average. Normal. Not bad. He sometimes gets them hotter, sometimes uglier. It depends on their level of enthusiasm, really. If there's anything that John loves, it's a good distraction. Unlocking a pretty girl's box is hard in the beginning because she doesn't want to give you the time of day. Ugly girls will let you talk for eons, only making life difficult when you finally try to get them naked, too worried to turn you off with their unshaven legs, bitty tits, and fleshy thighs. Different challenges. So long as they're screaming their pleasure in the end, it's a job well done.

The tip of his boot catches on the ankle of his other leg, and he trips a bit, but Miss Average is there to catch him. She acts like it's the most endearing thing in the world, saving what's left of his pride in the process.

And that's when Dustin walks by.

Fuuuuckin' Dustin.

John doesn't like him on the best of days. He used to be his neighbor and he *definitely* thinks John is cheating on his wife right now. The bastard's eyes widen before they narrow, and his lip curls a bit. John isn't cheating—hasn't for a while, please and thank you—though that doesn't change public perception. The guy doesn't know about the divorce, and why would he?

It's all John can do not to flip off his erstwhile neighbor as he tugs his lady friend close, wishing for the first time that she was sexy.

He stage-whispers, "Can we do it in your car?" then tips his chin up at fuckin' Dustin with a smarmy grin.

Yeah, you bastard. Think what you like, but we both know your wife is a frigid bitch. You just don't have the balls to do anything about it.

Forget that prick with his disdainful eyes. Fuck him, in fact. John's about to be whisked away from reality in the arms of a damsel, and that's what he'd like to focus on. Her chariot awaits.

Always their cars, never his. He doesn't want to sully it with their stains. And the fact that this random woman is rocking a hotrod that matches those pretty red nails makes fuckin' Dustin disappear from John's mind in a puff of asshole smoke. This woman's car is beyond stylish and sporty. It's a "put the top down and feel the wind in your hair" kind of machine. It's a "this costs more than a year of your salary" kind of machine. Consider *him* seduced, for God's sake.

She looks at the car with mischief in her eyes. "You wanna go for a ride?" The double meaning isn't lost on him one bit.

"You like to go fast in more ways than one, don't you?" He grins down at her. "Look who's full of surprises."

"Get in," she whispers into his neck, stepping away to unlatch the door before nudging him with nuzzles and non-kisses. Between the liquor and her hot breath, he thinks tonight might be salvageable after all.

Until he feels a deep stab in his neck.

He flails, but she shushes him and soothes, whispering, "You're mine now, John."

Frost runs through his veins, and something tastes funny. Metallic. Like pennies. His vision blurs and his hands paw with no grip.

And then he feels...

...he feels...

...

Losing Yourself

J ohn wakes up with a start, hissing in a quick breath as he rockets up, curling his shoulders to his knees by instinct to protect his soft belly. The light is still too bright after days with closed eyelids. Sealed eyelids. The thought makes him queasy. He feels the pinprick scabs as he rubs the thin strip of skin just above his lashes, grimacing. For some stupid reason, he's wondering if it will scar. His lips too. God knows he tried to scream more than enough to tear those little holes into little gouges. Somewhere inside, he knows he should be thinking more about the risk to his life versus his looks, but what can you do?

"You're awake," Kind-voice says. "How do you feel, big guy?"

"John," he repeats, his voice hard. "My name is *John.*"

"Say it again and I'll slap it out of you," the mean one hisses.

A slap is probably about all he could do, really. The two other men skulk around like naked, gangly skeletons. Terrifying, hollowed-out humans who refuse to identify themselves. Their dark hair is long, their patchy beards take over their faces, and their wild bushes hide flaccid disappointments. The only things that separate one from the other is that Kind-voice is dark-skinned with dreadlocks instead of the other one's peeling tan and white-boy bone structure. They also have different letters carved into their chests. The mean one's is a pale and ragged "H," long since scarred over. It looks shaky, like it took a few tries to dig it in deep enough. It bows together at the top, sloppy and haphazard. Kind-voice's is straighter by comparison. Sort of an "A" shape. John has an "A" too, though his is deep and red with surgical precision, a blocky font versus a triangular set of lines. It doesn't have the stitches that other parts of him oh-so-generously received, but it's deep enough to need them. He hadn't noticed the red slits with all his other body parts screaming, but now they're like a siren blaring over his heart. One that flashes, *Wrong, wrong, wrong!*

John tries a different tack. "Where are we?"

"Hell if I know," says the kind one with the other *A* centered over his breastbone. "Weather's good, that's all I can say. We don't freeze and we don't bake either, so long as we chase the sun."

John blinks at him. "What?"

Mister *A* points upward. The Fishbowl, as they call it, is a deep well that bows out at the bottom, flaring to either side like the flasks John once used in chemistry class, impressing girls with his mad scientist schtick.

"It's been cloudy lately, so it hasn't been an issue, but... See the lip of this place? It casts a sort of moving shadow, and it helps you hide from the sun. If you skirt the edges, you avoid the light, which means you'll also avoid a burn. I'd highly recommend, if you catch me. The sun beats on the altar almost all day, and if someone like you's not careful, you can red up, get heat stroke, or just outright blister."

"Altar?" John asks, his timbre higher than he'd like.

The skinny man grins, showing yellowed teeth. Some are broken, and John's mouth aches in sympathy. Mister *A* gestures center-stage where the large grate soaks up the sunlight. "The altar is where you do your business, as I'm sure you know by now."

Eyes narrowing, John looks at the thing with contempt. As long as he's been unconscious, he's not moved his bowels. His stomach says it's gonna happen, and it's gonna happen soon, but he has no desire to admit that bodily function even exists, never mind what he's going to have to do about it.

Mister *A* adds, "We also call it that because, when your stomach gets sick, that's where you go to pray." His lips quirk sarcastically. "It's also where the rainwater drains. There's a sewer below, but the water level's pretty far down."

"Can you get the grate up?" John asks, hope prickling him.

"Nah. And believe me, we've tried."

"Shut up," the mean one grunts, moving into the light. "Don't tell him anything." Mister ragged *H* seems feral, and his fist clamps down on something white—a knife, maybe? It looks like it's rough, but sharp. Made of stone or something. It must be what they used to pick apart the threads in his mouth. And his eyes.

John looks at the ground and does an instinctual risk-assessment. If things get scrappy, emaciated or not, that man could potentially do some damage before John could knock him down and out. What happens to stab wounds down here?

"You wanna know why else it's called the altar?" Mister *H* circles John in a slow and steady stalk. "It's because that's where sacrifices are made. Because almost no one who gets thrown down on the altar survives."

John feels like his eyes are burning holes in the stone floor as he cringes, remembering the screaming stranger. He wraps his arms around himself, thinking of that sickening crunch when the other man broke underneath the weight of John's fall. "I came down here with…someone. Where is he now?" Though John doesn't really want to know.

H spins on filthy, calloused heels, and John looks up to see him glaring. He seems both old and young at the same time. Alien. The hollows of his cheeks make every bone and sinew in his face visible, showing you exactly how all the pieces fit together. The sockets of his eyes are deep depressions, but the man's gaze is laser focused as he stares John down.

"You can't be that stupid." He narrows his eyes and hunkers, taking a beat before a wry smile curls his lips. "You're another plant, aren't you?"

"Shit. Will you stop already?" the other one groans.

H turns to his co-captive with a low warning. "She did it before."

Making a crude, one-finger gesture that would be amusing in any other circumstance, Mister *A* says, "Yeah? And how did that turn out for her? Why would she try it again? You think he's here to test us? Finish us off? Read us bedtime stories? Fuck you. Sometimes I think you want to be down here. That you think you *deserve* to be down here!"

Like an idiot, John scoffs. "And does he deserve to be down here?"

Vicious, *H* wheels back on him with a snarl. "I should have killed you when you touched down."

And John does something else he probably shouldn't. His patience snaps and he lunges forward, balling his fists and leaning over the man. He may not have eaten well for days, might still be on the last legs of his recovery, but he'll be damned if he lets himself be pushed around by a walking shadow.

"Well, you didn't, did you? And now it's too late. You wanna cut me? Try it. I'll break you in half, you feeble piece of shit. You might have been something once, but down here you're more useless than an ashtray on a motorbike. What the hell's your little whittling stick gonna do when I throw my knees on your spindle arms and wrap my hands around your throat? You gonna be able to cut me then? Huh? Even if you manage it, I'll just bleed on you first, then piss on your face when you're dead!"

H loses his balance, landing on his ass and looking at John with nothing but fury mixed with loathing—though fear lives there too. It's hidden under all that male bravado, but his wide eyes give him away.

"You both done?" Mister *A* asks simply. He looks at his co-captive. "See? He's strong. He's got meat on him that hasn't been eaten away yet. Energy reserves. He can do this."

H works his jaw, looking at the stone floor while John's face pulls into a sneer.

"I'm not doing anything for you."

"No?" Mister *A* asks mildly. "Not even help us try to get out of here? We're long overdue, pal." He gestures at his body. "As you've so kindly pointed out."

John feels like saying no again just to be an asshole. More than an asshole, though, he's a man of action. At least, he used to be. Or used to pretend to be.

Put up or shut up.

Shut up and do it.

Do until you do it right.

They need to escape. This is why they kept him alive. He'd known it; there's no surprise here. Still…

"Have you even got a plan? Or have you just sat back to rot this whole time?" If John can't take his anger out on the bitch who took him, it's got to go somewhere. "If you'd gotten out earlier, maybe I wouldn't be down here. Maybe there wouldn't have been people who were sacrificed on a fucking altar!"

What's left of *A*'s eyebrows lift. "Tell me, where were you three years ago, hmm? What were you doing? Who were you doing it with?"

John is immediately uncomfortable.

"Were you in a bed? Was your belly full? Or were you down here in a hole being tortured, starved, and having your mind fucked with every day? You haven't seen what I've seen! You haven't done what I've done just to survive!" *A*'s breath comes too fast as he lifts his arms, pointing to sores in his armpits that ooze with stink. He rubs just near them, and the skin sloughs off. "Look at me. Get a good eyeful. Think what you want, but at one point in my life, pal, I was you. And if you don't get with the program, you're going to be me sooner than you think."

After a heavy pause, *A* shakes his head and admits, "We're dying."

One look at them would say as much, but John still feels the weight of him saying it out loud.

"And I know you're not. We pulled some favors to keep you alive. We told her we needed someone to keep our minds sharp. We told her that we needed a friend."

"And I'm the 'friend.'" John can't keep the bitterness from his tone.

A's gaze turns hard. "Make no mistake, if not for us, you'd either be in that house getting worked up or you'd be just as dead as the guy you came down here with. We're not what got you into this mess, you are!"

John swallows, the last of the aches in his throat still complaining. He looks at his prison with new eyes, truly letting it in for the first time. You can't climb; the bell shape would put you nearly upside down. You'd have to be Spider-Man, but John's not seeing any of the necessary radioactive spiders. The walls and floor are made up of large clumps of masoned stone, cavernous and moist in places. The grate is rusted from years of human waste and the screws are covered with green lime, never to come out. There is a trough, too low and rickety to stand on, disgusting and mossy with barely any water left. His harsh judgment fades away. What the hell could they have possibly done to escape this place? What can they possibly do now?

Nothing.

His stomach sinks to his knees and his eyes mist with unshed tears. "There's no way out."

And that's when *A* grins. It's a gruesome, haunting thing.

Angry *H* curls in on himself, rocking and staring at John with wariness. "This is too soon. This is level five. He shouldn't be at level five."

"Yeah, well." *A* sighs and shakes his head, his smile unfaltering. "Necessity's a bitch, isn't it?"

"I thought it was the mother of all invention," John parries without thinking.

"That too." The other man nods. He takes a deep breath and lets it out with a puff before looking at John as if he's lost. "You promise you're not a plant?"

Feeling nothing but sorry for them, not even able to imagine what hellish things have gone on down here, John shakes his head. "I just want to go home." Even that empty den of nothing is better than this. Anything is better than this.

Mister *A* nods again, his stringy dreads bobbing. "Alright then." He walks to a place where the sun lights up the stone wall and points. "There."

John walks over and peers, not seeing anything special.

"That's where the ants come in. Some of them aren't worth talking about, but some are nice and fat." Mister *A* shrugs. "Protein."

John grimaces.

"But if they come in, that means they tunneled. Go. Look."

So, John does. Once close enough, he can see cracks in the

mortar. Hairline fractures in the mud that hold this place together.

"We can't go down," *A* says. "But maybe we can go up."

John fingers the line of crumbling material. "Give me the knife."

H immediately balks. "Over my dead body!"

"Sure," John replies evenly. "I'll wait. I promise I'll outlast you." Though he takes no pleasure in saying it this time around. He has no idea what this man was like before now, but here, in this place at this moment, his bark is worse than his bite.

The man's lip curls into a sneer. *H* doesn't say anything as he holds his only weapon up to his co-captive. Taking it gingerly, *A* passes it over, and John wastes no time in picking at the crack, stabbing deeper and rending the seam. His lips press together as he wiggles the rudimentary blade and starts to slide it unevenly. Sometimes it jumps forward, little chunks of cement and dust scattering down, other times he has to jostle and pry, but in the end, he gets his way around a whole stone, though he's already sweating and his hands ache. Looking at the others again, John can't blame them for being unable to do this.

He presses his palms down on the cool surface and...it shifts. John grins, the scabs on his mouth pulling open, though he doesn't care one bit. Using the knife again, he rocks it like a lever, widening the gap.

And that's when he hears the barking.

Wordlessly, *A* grabs his shoulders and does his best to spin John around. *H* is up too, eyes wide in panic and holding his palm out for his weapon, looking at John and silently pleading. Eyebrows knit, John hands it over and the others scatter to the shadows, nearly the opposite end of him.

That barking gets closer.

And closer.

Catching his eyes, *A* puts a finger to his lips in the universal *shh* gesture before clasping his hands in front of him as if in prayer. John nods, lifting his hand in turn and making the zip signal before staring at the circle of sunlight.

That's when he sees her. Nameless, just like them.

The Bitch.

"Feeding time!" her voice echoes.

A and *H* walk to the center of the Fishbowl, looking up into the sun with excitement filling their eyes and little smiles gracing their paper-thin faces, almost as if they're happy their master is home. Like animals. Like pets.

And maybe that's exactly what they are.

———

At this point, John has blunted the blade. Every time he hands it back, the oh-so-angry Mister *H* glares at John like he murders puppies for a living, but John has grown immune to the man's attitude at this point. So many phrases of rhetoric stick in his mind, and he has to hold his breath to stop them from spewing out. The "To change your life, change your attitude" sort of shit. It makes him hate himself in silence.

He wrenches a piece of jerky in his teeth, chewing through the tough meat. "No vegetables? Fruit?"

The kind Mister *A* scoffs at him. "No. Vitamins though. Bread sometimes. If we're good."

"The salt helps your body hold water," *H* mutters, hunkered on the far edge of the rounded wall. John has no idea if that's true or not.

Jaw aching, he sighs at his handiwork. Nodding at the wall, he says, "Problem one might be a checkmark, I think. I got the rock out last night while you were sleeping"—though it had hurt his road-rashed body to do it—"and I'm able to put it back in pretty smooth. Can't even tell it moved, can you?"

The other men look at it, then at him, one like he's a God, the other like he doesn't believe him for a minute. John promises himself that he'll show off his hard work later when he's sure it's safe. One member of his audience can praise him, the other can eat crow.

"Problem two is that there's no way we can fit," John continues. "The surrounding rocks are set more firmly so they're harder to get out, if I can get them out at all. I have no idea what will happen to the..." He gestures with pursed lips. "I dunno, structural integrity of this place if I keep picking at it."

Mister *A* shakes his head. "The wall is pinned pretty good. Look." He points. "Most rocks are offset, so they'll hold each other together. Distributes the weight or something, I think."

"That's the problem," *H* grumbles into his hands. "You think. You don't *know*. What happens if we ruin it? What do you think she'll do to us then?"

John can't help but grin. "We'll just tell her it's her fault for building such a shitty well."

His co-captives' horrified looks ruin his good mood.

"I don't see how you can joke about this." *H* shakes his head.

"What can I say? I'm an optimist."

"Or just plain stupid!"

"Ignorant," *A* corrects softly. He shakes his head back and forth, the gesture so slight it's almost unseen. "You don't know what happens when you break the rules."

John lets that thought sink in for a minute before dismissing it completely. He doesn't want to hear about any rules. That means he'd have to sit in the moment and process what he's really doing. What's really happening. Instead, he stares at his stone, focused and hard. *That's* where he wants his mind to be. Having something to put his energy into. Distraction and action is his thing, but every now and then, reality hits. Only then does he feel the pain in his body. Does he truly look at where he is and who he's with. Does he let himself see the terrible bleakness of *now.* But then his stubbornness kicks in again. And his pride.

Fuck that bitch.

"Let's call her lovely reaction 'problem number three' for now. No use thinking about that until it happens." For all John knows, he can get them out of there sooner rather than later. "Problem four. The dirt."

The others stare off, expressions vacant. They get like this sometimes. Zombified. A stupor or something. John snaps his fingers and their heads about-face into attention mode.

"Problem. Four." John ticks his jaw to the side with annoyance. He hates repeating himself, no matter how much money it makes him. "What do I do with the dirt?"

"The altar," *A* states the obvious.

"Not what I mean." John shakes his head. "You guys are... disgusting, let's be honest." He's met with harsh glares. "But not one of us is outright caked in mud. What's behind there is wet and deep and dark. We start digging and hauling, it's gonna show."

"I can't dig and haul," *H* confesses. It comes out soft with shame. After a second, he flicks his matted, overlong hair over his shoulder and hardens up. "Because I don't want to."

A just laughs at his co-captive's idiocy and gets up to take a piss. The man has no qualms about it, having done this—for all intents and purposes—since time immemorial. Zero B.F. Before Fishbowl.

John's quick to look at his wall again. He mostly tries to keep his eyes on their faces to ignore their nudity. He tries even harder to ignore his own and the self-consciousness that comes with it. It's not like he's incomparable—puts them to shame, in his honest opinion—but swinging in front of male strangers was never his idea of a good time. He's not a prude, really he's not, and it's not like he's never stood next to someone at a urinal before, but watching this man's black ass clench as he tips his hips forward is as terrible as it is eye-drawing. A sort of "I want to look because I'm not supposed to look." Like checking out pretty girls when you're already married.

He cuts off that train of thought as the scent of ammonia fills the air.

"We need to ration the water harder," *A* says, as if that wasn't an issue already. "New Guy hauls the dirt and tosses it down, and we keep enough to the side for him to wash his hands."

"We have the bucket," *H* admits. "But it's for fresh water. He'll muck it up."

And honestly, John will need to wash more than just his hands. His arms and chest at the very least, and that's if he's careful. He's not going to argue at this point though. They seem less than with it, so this little line item can happily slip their minds for now.

John asks, "How often does she...I dunno...water us?" For lack of a better term.

H raises his eyebrows almost playfully and chuckles. "Depends on her mood."

Now it's John's turn to say, "I fail to see why that's amusing. We need water more than food. It's, like, lesson one in elementary health class. 'Your body is ninety-percent water,'" he lilts in a nasal, sarcastic, yet instructive voice.

"Sixty percent," Mister *A* corrects, shaking himself off. "Depending on your age." Looking over his shoulder and rubbing his hands mindlessly over his jutting hips, he adds, "That's what she tells us anyway."

John huffs. "The bitch."

"Shut your fucking mouth." *H*'s eyes dart up to the lip of the well and back down again, pinning John with a pointed stare.

"What? Is not insulting her a rule now too?"

"You have no idea." It comes out as a whisper, and John's not entirely sure who said it.

He clears his throat. "Problem five." John points up at the ring of sunlight. "Cujo."

"Cujo." Good old Mister *A* snickers, scratching at the letter on his chest.

"It's colored like a rottie, from what I can tell," John says, "and from the way it snarls at night, I'm guessing it's not a happy thing."

"Probably catching rabbits," *H* thinks aloud.

"I'd like to catch rabbits," *A* says with a dreamy look on his face. "At this point, though, I'd eat the grass." His laugh is completely mirthless. Looking at John, he smiles—genuine, yellowed, and terrible. "This is nice, you know."

Flabbergasted isn't the right word, but it comes close. "Nice?"

"Being with someone new. Having...hope, I guess. Something to do. Something to talk about. It makes this place more..." He waves his hand, looking for a word.

"Bearable," *H* adds, quiet again.

"Yeah. That."

John doesn't feel that sentiment in any way but chooses, wisely, to keep his mouth shut. "Does she come every day?"

"Unpredictable." *A* sighs. "Again, it depends on her mood. And on how nice we're being. She needs us to be nice."

"Of course she does," John grumbles. "Day or night?"

A squints upward, pursing his lips. "Day mostly. Dinnertime maybe. Never really too deep into the dark. She doesn't like looking down here with the flashlight, I don't think."

"She wants us to see her." *H* curls his knees up to his chest, covering his scar.

John fingers his own healing wound, scabbed over but puffy and red all around the edges. "What are these, anyway?" he asks.

Mister *A* rubs his marked breastbone, a strange look on his face. "Scarlet letters."

Horror spiders across John's skin, leaving gooseflesh in its wake. He's read that book. It's been a long time, but it's always hovered in the back of his mind. "A for Adultery."

He's met with a hushed voice and a nod. "I told you it was your own fault you were down here."

John tics his jaw up at his resident bully. "Why is yours different? What does H mean?"

He grimaces. "Mine's an A too... She just didn't know how to do it right yet."

John's stomach twists. She's gotten better with practice, evidently. "How many have there been?"

A hesitates before saying, "We've lost count. They don't always end up down here, but they don't usually last long when they do. They come and go, if not in one way, then another. All except you." He eyes John carefully before looking at *H* with his mouth drawn in a grim, straight line. "Us, though? We were the first two. Him. Then me. We've been here from the beginning. And no matter what it took, we survived."

Again, and desperately, John tries, "Tell me your names."

But, again, he is told: "Names don't matter down here."

THE PAST -
INTERLUDE SEVEN

Losing himself, John is knuckles deep inside some unknown stranger from some unknown bar. One he'll never go back to. Her car has fuzzy seats he's more than happy to let her ruin in all her open-legged splendor. She's at his complete mercy—all cries and stifled moans, one foot planted on the roof of the interior, the other flung over the passenger's seat—but John is thinking more about the rain on his ass than anything else. Half in, half out of the car, he's in a pretty compromising position.

She'd parked in the dusty, paper bag brown dirt behind the building. It was on the later side of the night, making it the perfect opportunity for sex under the stars. Unfortunately, they didn't both fit in her compact piece of trash, and the sky opened up with its own plans. Now John's pants are flagging as his mouth gets to work. His belt sags a bit over his crack and exposes him to the cold droplets of doom. He's probably been losing too much weight. His steady diet of beer hasn't quite caught up to his brutal exercise routine. After all, it doesn't matter if hell itself rises from the bowels of the Earth, he's still got to look the part he's cast himself in. Simply: A Success

Story. It's a refrain that's getting tired and old. Going out of fashion. And it's not really working anymore either.

He lifts his eyes but can barely see her over the haze of his stupor and the soft curve of her belly. It doesn't matter. The more pressing concern is whether or not he has the ability to *perform* at this particular point of his inebriation. That hovering threat of embarrassment sticks in his brain like a nail in a wall. That and wondering what it's going to feel like when he finally sits down in his rain-sogged trousers. The whole situation kind of pisses him off. How dare the sky quite literally rain on his parade?

Maybe this whole thing was a bad idea. Or maybe he should just try to hike his body further into the car...but no. Then the angle he's using to suckle her would be all wrong. With the way she pants and mewls, she's got to be close, and if he can get her off in spite of everything, he'll call that a win.

Pulling back for a gasp of less-than-fresh air, he watches his handiwork, and it makes him smirk. Still, he can see the tan line where his wedding ring has left him bleached, and suddenly that draws more attention than his fluttering fingers. His rhythm becomes sloppy, but she's too far gone to complain. They're both in the bag tonight. Maybe that's why he can't get her over the edge.

But then he manages it a few seconds later, and his grin doubles as she lays limp, blissed out with thighs trembling.

Still got it, baby.

He kisses her knee as a distraction more than anything as he sneaks her keys off her seat. Those are going happily to the bartender who, in turn, will happily order her a ride. No driving and dying in her condition, please and thank you. He may be an asshole, but life is life, and life is precious, even when you're wasting it in the back seat of a dirty car on the wrong side of thirty with a woman you barely know, and don't want to.

The heavy wooden entryway is identical to every other dive bar he's ever seen. It opens to invite him into the din, letting him listen to the blare of yet another pop song he only knows the chorus to. John works his way toward the glossy semi-circle that keeps the addicts an arm's length from their liquid vice, and waggles the keys in front of the bartender to get his attention. The jangle is barely audible over the latest verse of sexual euphemisms.

The burly, middle-aged man lifts his bristle-brush eyebrows and gives John a knowing look. "That was quick."

John shrugs. "I found myself only servicing the lady this evening."

The guy narrows his eyes. "She alright?"

The bartender doesn't know him from Adam, so John doesn't blame him for being concerned about his lady patron. If anything, it warms John's heart.

"She's more than all right, I'd think." He winks, throwing a bit of his smarmy charm around before accidentally rocking on the balls of his feet.

He's on the receiving end of a sigh. The bartender holds out his hand for her keys, and then once more for good measure. "Yours too."

"Nuh-uh," John *tsk*s. "I'm walking. I'm close by."

"Alright. Your friend has five minutes to come back looking for these before I call the cops."

"Seriously?" John balks for only a second, giving up near-immediately and lifting his hands in surrender. "Fine, fine. I'll go escort her back in, how's that?"

"Seems like the gentlemanly thing to do."

John is about to open the door again when it does it by itself. The lady of the hour looks at him, absolutely livid. "WHERE THE FUCK ARE MY *KEYS!?*"

And his grin resurfaces. Looking at the bartender, he says, "Isn't she a peach?"

———

He hates the electric *bing-bong* that announces his entry into the 24/7 drug store almost as much as he hates the bright fluorescents that threaten to blind him.

Living close by was a stellar fib, one he'd delivered perfectly if he says so himself. Still, life is life, and he's not an idiot. Not entirely, anyway. He'd walked a bit and pinged for an Uber, more than happy to be carted away like Cinderella after a very productive ball. Midnight has come, and he's a pumpkin once more, if by pumpkin you mean a sobering drunk picking up a nice, big bottle of ibuprofen along with his other medical necessities. Much to his chagrin. The truth is that he's on a lot of pills now. He's lost track of how many. They go in a neat little row of boxes, one for each day, and he downs them mindlessly before bed. Some for anxiety, some for depression, some for sleep. Some that are a mix of all three. Peace, happiness, and lies in a bottle. Lies that tell others that he's still got it. That he's still the success he's always been. That he's still someone worth admiration. The mask is slipping though, and his wallet slips out of his pocket with it as he gets ready to pay for his little slice of sanity.

The late-night pharmacy cashier is cute. Cuter than she should be for...whatever this job is. Retail? Some mix of that and medical? What the hell do you do to earn a job behind the magical counter where all the ways to numb yourself live?

"This one is new to your list of prescriptions," she tells him. "Do you have any questions for the pharmacist? I can get her to call you when she's in tomorrow."

John leans forward a little, still a bit drunk but holding it in nicely. He glances at her name tag. "Aren't *you* the pharmacist, Miss Catherine?"

Maybe it's his straight teeth that makes her smile back at him, tucking her hair behind her ear. "Not yet. Soon."

John eases out his credit card in a familiar, well-worn slide. He'd take his flirtation further, but he's too close to home and he's already proven that his dick doesn't work tonight. "What's the damage?"

She plucks his card from his hand and rams it, chip-side up, into the little machine he was supposed to use himself. "One-hundred and seventy dollars."

Even with his mega-insurance too. This country sucks.

"Just another one of the ongoing costs of being alive." He sighs, pressing green buttons that ask him to donate to causes he doesn't bother looking at. Yes and yes and fine and whatever until he's spent about seven extra bucks on his nonchalance.

"Tell me about it," she commiserates. "At least you don't have pink tax."

"Ahh, the lady's cost of being a lady." He feigns sympathy. Before she goes into a rant about the price of a maxi pad, he leans in one last time. "Some pink tax is a scam though. Waxing. Razors. I prefer my women unshaven." A bold-faced lie if there ever was one. "Find yourself a guy like me and save yourself a bit of money and a lot of time."

She blushes beautifully and his smarmy grin returns. He shifts his gaze away, pretending to be ashamed of himself. "I'm sorry, that was a bit much, wasn't it?"

She bites her lip and there's a slight curve to the corners of her mouth. "It's alright. Maybe I'll take your advice. I could search the database for someone actually in my generation who's on this same impressive laundry list of psych meds. Then I'll just keep my eyes open for one that's as generous and free-thinking as you are."

That's gotta be a HIPAA violation of some kind. He covers his chest as if in a mock stabbing. "Ouch, Miss Catherine! For so many reasons, ouch! Though also, touché! I suppose I earned that."

Her giggle is sweet and innocent. "I'll give you a pass. You look like you've had a rough night." Which means he looks like shit.

She hands him the top of his overlong receipt, and he marvels at how it just keeps spewing from the printer, bar code after bar code of coupons he'll never even look at, let alone use. "I'll, ah..."—he starts to fold it into an unfortunate rectangle/ball—"recycle this."

Even though he knows he can't. He saw a whole show about it. There are things you think you can throw into that pretty green recycling bin, but most of the time you're wrong. And when you're wrong, you contaminate whatever else is in the bottle-filled bucket, making it useless. The show called this optimistic ignorance *Wish*-cycling. John had thought it was a clever concept and plagiarized the fuck out of it for a hot minute before he realized nobody cared. The cashier grins at him like he's a good citizen though, and that's all he was really going for.

He nods politely as he walks out, feeling his hypocrisy down to his bones. He doesn't care one bit about saving the world. He'll be long gone before it burns, and he's the only one that really matters anymore anyway.

Suffering

The Bitch doesn't feel like helping today, it seems. No matter how much the decrepit Misters *A* and *H* try to get her attention, her sympathy, they are summarily denied. That means no food, no water, just her gazing down on them with her eyebrows knit and tears in her eyes, her fingers caressing the edges of the rough stone lip of the well. John understands why this place is called the Fishbowl. The Bitch hovers, watching them vacantly, enjoying them milling around and moving their mouths at her.

John's fear has taken a back seat, his rage boiling just under the surface instead, as furious as he is ravenous. They'd long since run out of meat, and the bread she'd offered yesterday with a smile on her face had been gone before she even finished walking away.

Cujo whines and barks at The Bitch's heels, likely begging for the treat John will not get. It jumps up, and the nails on its paws make clicking noises against the stones above as it pants, backlit and slobbering everywhere. John still can't tell what kind of dog it is, he only knows that he feels both jealous and indignant every time he looks at the animal. Moping, he thinks petulant thoughts like, *How dare it run around like that?* as if the animal was doing it to personally offend him. Irrational. It's all so irrational.

John tries to assess the dog. Size. Potential strength. Potential number of teeth he'll have to contend with. Cujo's nightly rabbit hunting tends to result in snarls, grunts, and ripping flesh. John imagines he hears the bunnies squeal, but tells himself it's only his imagination playing tricks on him. He's not even sure bunnies *can* squeal. Still, he's terrified to be on the receiving end of that vicious attack. If it happens—when it happens—will it be with the creature's jaws wrapped around his face, or some other part of his body? God save his dick.

"Come on, sweetheart," *H* says, making John's fury near-incandescent. "Why are you so sad? You can tell us."

One of the rules John has inferred: you never ask for food. If you ask, you get less than you would have otherwise. It seems you can't ask for water either, but you *can* feign hoarseness and see if she picks up on it and/or cares. Instead of screaming at her, the dying men pretend to worship her. Anything to get her to laugh. To smile. To coo and talk at them. To want them to live another stupid, useless, heart-wrenching day.

The other men put on fetid smiles and praise her sweetness as if she were a goddess. Sometimes, John doesn't think *H* is faking it. Sometimes he thinks the man really believes the words he spews. The way he looks at her is just a little too intense, a little too earnest. It makes John's skin crawl. Is this what Stockholm syndrome looks like?

A heavy, feminine exhale is all *H* gets for his efforts, so *A* tries instead. "You were so happy yesterday. Did something happen at work? Something at home? How can we help you, darling?"

John wants to tear their tongues out but does his best to

hold his own, hunkering down out of the light of the sun and watching them watch each other.

She shifts, resting her face on the palm of her hand and sighing out the word, "John...?" with something like longing.

His hackles rise. Surely she doesn't want him to join in on this disgusting, sycophantic parade. But he's hungry. He's starving.

Fucking head games.

H tries to speak again, but John does what he's told. An old childhood adage: Speak when spoken to.

"Yes? Can I" *kill you, you goddamned bitch?* "do anything for you? I mean, there are limits to what I can do from down here," bitterness creeps in and he smooths it out quickly, "but I can at least listen."

He's sulking. He knows he's sulking. *H* is glaring at him with deep disgust. He's fucking this up, he knows, but he's not a mindless automaton ready to roll over and take everything she gives him quite yet. Maybe it will come, or maybe he'll get them out first. Only time will tell.

She laughs, but it's more like a grumpy *harrumph* than its usual sweet sound. "Why would I talk to you?" she asks, disdain dripping from her lips.

He clears his throat. "You've got to talk to someone, so it might as well be me. Us," he corrects, looking at the others.

She mopes like a teenager. "I don't wanna talk to you."

Then maybe you should go the fuck away, he seethes. He keeps that well-practiced softness in his voice. "Then who do you want to talk to?" *A therapist? Preferably a jury. Or an executioner?*

She twiddles her fingers again. "John?"

"What?" He wants to snap at her, he really does, instead he tries to say it like a lover.

Her faraway gaze hardens. "Shut up."

And he flinches. The others face her but are eyeing him in

their peripheral vision. *H* pushes his matted hair over his shoulder and tries to salvage whatever John is doing wrong.

"Maybe you just need a nap, baby girl. You always feel better after a nap."

It's then that her face twists and the tears spill over. "I'm so lonely!" she cries, pressing her face into her hands and shaking it back and forth. "I don't know what to do! Do you think I need to go get someone else? Will that make me feel better? Will that make *you* feel better?"

A cold dread falls over John, catching in his throat like a rock.

"No, sweetheart. We have a new friend now. You gave that to us. We don't need anyone else." *H* shifts his stance, edging closer to the center of the well. "If you're lonely, stay with us. You don't have to talk. You don't have to do anything." He casts a glance at *A* and smirks before looking up at her with a shit-eating grin. "You wanna watch us fight?"

She peeks up over her hands and *A*'s gaze drops to the ground for a minute. When he meets her eyes again, his smile is soft. "I can give it a shot if that's what you want, darlin'."

She cocks her head to the side like a dog who doesn't quite understand a command. Scrubbing her eyes, she *hmms* and flicks her eyes at John. "Do you guys want to fight him?"

He has chills.

Please don't ask me to do it. If I fight them, I'll break them. They're like matchsticks. They're like porcelain dolls. They're like dry sand sculptures.

"I don't want to hurt them," John says. It sounds too much like begging for his liking.

She toys with her hair and *harrumphs* again.

"I can take him." *H* winks at her playfully. "He's a big guy, but I'm wily. I think I've got a chance. What say you, baby girl?"

She giggles and John hates her. He hates her, he hates her, he hates her.

H walks over with a cocky swagger and lifts his eyebrows slightly, cracking his knuckles. John's first thought is that this is going to hurt his ego more than his body. The sad part is, he's right.

When the punch comes, it's almost like a slap. John plays a good sport and lets his head rock to the side. The question now: Is he supposed to hit the man back? And if so, will he? And if he does, how much damage is it going to do?

He pretends he's an actor and leaves his head to the side for a moment while glaring daggers at the skeleton who thwacked him. His fists clench, unsure of what to do next. When he lifts them in front of his face, it's defensive more than anything else, but—

"No, no!" she yells down, frantically waving her hands in front of her. "Don't hurt him! Stop! I didn't say you got to fight back!" She sniffles. Her hair hangs down in pigtail braids as she tips herself farther over the lip of the well, the sun making a little line of light around her body. "Hey. Are you guys thirsty?"

"Yes," all three say in unison.

She smiles. "Okay. I'll get the bucket."

The *bucket* is just that. Something plastic you buy at the grocery store when you feel like mopping old-school versus breaking out the Roomba or the Swiffer. It comes down on a twined bit of plastic rope, strong and somehow sharp, like if it ran through your hands too fast, you wouldn't only get a friction burn, your hands would bleed.

There are lugging grunts and sloshes as she sets it up on the rim and starts to loop the rope around the arched handle. Not for the first time, John is terrified of what will happen if the rope slips and she douses them. Will she laugh and go get them more, or will she sulk and run away, leaving them to lick their dirty fingers just to soften their rough, whitened tongues?

All three of them lift their arms as if they're welcoming God into their embrace. John is the tallest, John is the strongest, so John gets a hold of it first. The bucket is cleaner than anything in this place, so it's extra cruel when she ticks her chin to the side and reminds John harshly, "The trough."

He grimaces, looking at the mossy thing and pouring the bucket in. Oliver Twist screams in his mind, *Please, sir, can I have some more?!* But he's already been well schooled on that. One of the few rules they've told him outright. He walks back to the center and holds the bucket as high as he can just to make the fucking thing easier for her to lift out.

"Keep it," she says. "Just undo the rope." Meaning she's too damn lazy to lug up a two-pound pail.

"Thank you, sweetheart," *H* coos.

John suddenly wants to clock him. His cheek barely stings, but his soul does.

———

There is a special kind of suffering that comes from a lack of food and water. Your body hurts, sure, but that's to be expected. The funny thing is when it doesn't anymore. John never really expected that. At first, your stomach yells "I hate you" for days on end, but eventually it gives up and just becomes a low mutter. A petulant grumble. The thirst, though, that always stays. Which is why it's so terrible that they're setting aside part of what they have to drink in order to wash off John's secret sin: the dirt and loam that he grabs handfuls of at night, desperate not to let any fall to the floor. There are no brooms to cover his tracks, after all. As he goes deeper, his arms come dangerously close to running over the moist soil, which would stain him for sure. He gets it on his forearm once and nearly bursts into tears. His mind is a never-ending loop of the word *careful.*

That's the worst part of all this. It's not only about the deep-seated need for food and water. It's not only about the intense shame of how quickly John has become exactly like his co-captives when it comes to cow-towing to The Bitch and her whims. What really gets him, deep down inside, is that he's become completely irrational. At times, it's like he's incapable of coherent thought. And he's not alone in his stupors either. The two men who suffer with him fall into silences and waking-nothingness. It was scary at first, but now he's learned all he needs to do is snap his fingers in front of them to get their attention. It's getting his own that's the problem.

That's what he does now, flicking his fingers together in clipping snips, looking down on them and lonely for conversation. "You guys ever see *Survivor*?" he asks, standing and leaning against the cool stone, taking a small break from his mini-hauls, dirt caked under his nails.

"What?" *H* asks, startling out of a snooze.

"The TV show?" *A* chimes in, lifting his head from his knees and coughing a bit. It's wet and worrying. John wonders if he got him sick.

John nods a bit, a small smile gracing his face. "Yeah. The one where they throw something like thirty people on a deserted island and say, 'Good Luck. Don't die and you might win a million dollars!'"

A snorts. "At least they had a water well, if I remember correctly."

"And rice," John agrees.

"Don't talk to me about rice," *H* groans, mournful and longing.

"See," John starts, taking a deep breath. "I always thought

those people were so stupid. Not because they went on the island, but because, after a while, they couldn't do the simplest of things. They'd get a few episodes in and start making these idiotic mistakes. They'd get uselessly paranoid or stop performing well in challenges or become super-PMS-level emotional. You tell yourself, 'Yeah, they haven't eaten, that must be it. I get it.' But you don't." John's eyes burn, wanting to cry but unable. Whether it's because he won't let them or because his body won't spare the moisture, he's not sure. "Now I sit here, paranoid, even though I know it's somewhere in the middle of the night and she's dead asleep. If there's a change in the goddamn wind, I put that stone back as fast as I possibly can. I've picked that thing up and put it down so much I should be a bodybuilder by now. And the more I slim down, the harder it gets. How long until it's too hard to do at all?

"I smell the dirt and I literally think about eating it. Or squeezing it to get a few drops of water out or something. I feel like crying all the time. Or raging. Or shutting down. It's hard to move, hard to think. I feel like my brain is melting."

A and *H* say nothing. John realizes his spiel is worthless. Preaching to the choir, only the choir has no sympathy. They've been down here much longer than he has, after all.

In *Survivor*, they only stayed on the island for thirty days. How does he compare? How pathetic is he compared to the champions he watched and judged for hours on end?

"How many days have I been down here?" he asks. "I don't even know."

"Get used to it," *A* says, a bit on the raspy side before coughing a little again. "They all look the same. Even the seasons barely change, except for the rain. And you don't want to be here for the rain."

That would happen on the island too. Cold, huddling,

and shivers. Misery and despair on tap as they did their best to sleep amidst a raging storm with no shelter.

John idly wonders what the contestants would dream about while suffering in the elements. Lately, his dreams have shown visions of him and his co-captives eating a huge meal together in the sunlight, like they do on the rewards part of the show. A special sort of feast just for being well-behaved little ass kissers, so good at their only job. Sometimes it's so vivid, it's painful. He can taste the food, and there's often booze too. The better the dream, the more it hurts when you wake up. He'd rather have nightmares.

"We're going to die down here, aren't we?" *H* asks, quiet. He gets that way sometimes. Depressed. If he's not raging or flirting or *nothing,* he's sad. He goes back and forth between hating the plan because he thinks she'll kill them if she finds out, hating the plan because he thinks it will never work, and hating the plan because it *is* working but not fast enough.

"No. I'm going to get us out." John states this as firmly as he can before righting himself. Break time is over. He reaches into his undersized hole of hope and grabs a double fistful of dark brown dirt, smooshing it into itself and packing it down before carefully bringing it center stage and stuffing it down through the grate of the altar.

He goes back and tries to compress the dirt against the walls of the tunnel as well, smashing it and widening the hole as much as he can. They loosened another rock, but even once they get it out all the way, this is still going to be too tight of a fit. John doesn't consider himself claustrophobic but getting through this is going to require that he morph into an enormous, man-shaped worm. The thought terrifies him. The question posed is: Would he rather be buried alive trying to escape, or rot in an open, spacious tomb?

"Can I help you?" *A* asks yet again. He's tried. He really has.

"No," John tells him once more, but gently this time. "We don't have enough water to wash you up," is what he says, but the real reason is that *A* tires out way too fast, and the last time he spent hours curled in a little ball while dry-weeping. John had to keep working through the whole thing, ignoring the man's hollow cries. It was one of the most heartbreaking experiences of his life.

The man coughs again and swallows it, probably too tired to get up and hock it down into the sewer. Would The Bitch give them more meds, like she did for him? Can they pull any more favors from their evil overlord without repercussions? John's not sure. And because he's not sure, all he can do is keep digging.

———

H is standing against the secret wall, idly wiggling his blade into the mortar that surrounds the rock that's next in line, just to the right of the excised bricks John so carefully tucks back into place. It seems like the best one to try, so John's happy to let *H* have at it. He's getting almost nowhere though, barely making any progress, but every little bit helps. The Bitch came by a little bit ago and caught him, but he just acted like he was honing the knife's edge. She'd asked him why he was doing it and he'd grinned at her.

"In case you ever really want me to get in a fight, princess."

She'd laughed then. It sinks into John's head that *H* may have fought before. Maybe a lot. Maybe he's killed people. The thought makes him shudder.

It's twilight now and the crickets are chirping as *H* toys with the wall, making little scraping sounds. The stars are out, and John can almost see the Milky Way floating above them. It makes him think of astronauts. Discovery. A vast universe of millions of possibilities. Yet here he is, in an area of about two hundred square feet in circumference, and it might as well be all that exists.

"What is she like?" John asks. "She's bipolar, obviously. Sadistic, absolutely. An absolute c—"

"Shut up," *H* hisses, just like always. Probably afraid to get caught. All three of them spend most of their day afraid to get caught.

A is squatting over the altar, letting out what little his intestines have to offer. John's still not used to it, can barely do it himself. *A* tells him he has a shy asshole, but that he better get over it soon or he'll tear himself a new one when it finally comes out in little rock-hard pellets. Actually, John's pride has given way to his bodily functions, but only when he's positive they're asleep. Their soft sawing of wood is his gut's cue to make shit happen, quite literally. Their snores are evenly spaced with the occasional snort that indicates either sinus issues or nightmares, but John doesn't think they wake up. Either that, or they're doing a fine job letting him pretend he still has his dignity. Though, honestly, he didn't really have much left to begin with.

"I cheated on my wife with her," *A* says out of nowhere, and John sits straight up, snapping to attention. *H* tenses and stabs his knife into the mortar with a grunt. *A* goes on as if he hadn't heard. "She talked to me about it a lot back then. Cheating. Why I did it, what I felt like when I did it. Was it the sin of it that got me off, or was it the danger of getting caught? I didn't really know, actually. She was like my freaking therapist when we laid down together after…well…*after*. She kept me going with her for about two months. I would sneak away or 'work late' as often as I could during the week, and when I talked, she would listen.

"Idiotically, I fell in love with her. Head over heels kinda thing. It was only then that I got my answer. I cheated because my wife never listened, she only talked. But *her*...she listened. She was fascinated by me. She made me feel like the world revolved around me. And then she put me down here. Now my world revolves around her."

H goes on another small stabbing spree and each *thunk* into the wall makes *A* flinch.

John desperately wants to know *H*'s story as well, but he won't ask. It may not be a real rule, but it is one anyway. If not out of necessity, out of kindness. To be fair, John doesn't want to tell them his story either.

"How many others do you think she's done this to?" John asks. "How many have you seen? What happens to them when they come down here?"

If *A*'s going to open up, let him open up wide.

The man has already finished his business, but he just squats there and dries. It's the best they can do. He grins bitterly. "Well, some of them went *snap-crackle-pop* when they landed, just like the guy you smashed to death."

John's heart drops, pushing his lungs down somewhere around his groin. He doesn't want to think about that. He doesn't want to talk about that. The screaming stranger was a fever dream as far as he's concerned. Not his fault.

Refusing to accept responsibility and therefore unchastised, he can't help but dig deeper. "Have you ever killed anyone?"

H huffs out a dark laugh, his forehead resting against the stone as he chips away. "You really want to know the answer to that, or are you just trying to ease your own conscience?"

John scowls. "I really want to know. I want to know what we're in for."

Standing up, *A* works his way over to the far wall, snuffing back snot and clearing his throat. "For better or for worse, we do whatever she tells us to, whatever that means in the moment." He slides down the wall and curls around his knees, rocking a little. His eyes are far, far away, and his face is a mask of unreadable silence and sores.

"It's one of the rules," *H* nods. "One of the ones you can never break."

"Ever," *A* agrees, but it's not scared or sad. It's haunted. And resigned.

THE PAST - INTERLUDE SIX

"I'm home!" John calls from just inside the door, already slipping off his shoes in the entryway.

Heading into the living room, the couches are beautiful to look at. Works of modern art. Coming into money has made John a bit pretentious, and the fact that the designer of his couch has an iconic name that is known in the industry versus a forgettable something-cheap from Joe Schmo's Discount Emporium stokes John's ever-growing pride. If the people he led like sheep heard his elite sofa's name, they wouldn't even know what it was, but once he hits some magic inner circle, he knows someone will. That impressive, charismatic, future person will say, "I have something from that collection as well," then it would be worth the godawful price tag. Too bad it's so damn uncomfortable.

Beth sits on the edge of it, staring intently at their similarly distinctive coffee table. A beautiful set with matching end tables, all of which belong in a magazine. Rather than looking at the fantastic glass surface, John stares at what's on it. A key. A single key. It's black and emblazoned with a little Hello

Kitty, making his heart wrench painfully. Its white face and pastel pink bow are slightly rubbed off from years of use, and John hates it on sight. He doesn't bother to put his own keys down. He has a feeling where this is going.

Beth's red hair hangs around her face in little tendrils. Her makeup is damn near perfect and her clothes wrap her sweet curves like a dream. It's like she's putting on a show for him one last time. He'd offer to unwrap her like a gift, but his chest and ribs are covered with the stains of another woman's kisses, and he thinks she probably knows it.

She doesn't bother looking at him. She just says, "So," in a voice that's so bland, it's like this moment doesn't matter. With that word, she slips off her rings. Those are on the cheap side. He'd never replaced them for her. She hadn't wanted him to—was almost offended that he'd offered, ranting about sentimental value and all that. Still, his heart aches to see that bit of history fall to the table as she drops them with clinks and clatters.

"I know you cheat," she tells him. It's in the same tone of voice one would use to say, *Do you want to watch the news?* "I also know you've been cheating since it happened."

"I won't talk about that," he warns her, voice tighter than he means it to be.

It's only then that she looks at him. "I thought you'd get it out of your system. I thought I'd give you a pass. I shut down, you amped up. We coped in our own ways. But...day by day, sign by sign, I fell out of love with you."

He opens his mouth, and she cuts him off.

"It's not a matter of saying you're sorry. You're not sorry at all. You're too focused on *overcoming.*" She growls it like the insult it's meant to be. "This failure is just one more thing you can try to overcome. It'll sell more books. Get more gigs. More women."

He looks at his own wedding ring, the one he'd traded up for, not the one he married her with. It's not a lie to say that he loves his wife. He loves her very much, in a different sort of way. She's a comfort to come home to because she knows his favorite meals and is willing to suffer through TV shows she hates with her ankles draped over his lap, keeping his thighs warm. But he hates her a little too. Is that why he does what he does? Maybe. More than that, though, it's because it's exciting. Because, for some unknown reason, nothing quite does it for him like these random nameless, faceless encounters with women who look at him like he's the answer to all their problems. And he believes that, in a very real, tangible way, he just might be.

Leaning back against their uncomfortable piece of furniture-art, Beth's hands clasp each other loosely. "I don't hate you, John. But I don't want you either."

No one has ever said that to him. Not since high school anyway. Even then, she was the one who said it, and he'd wooed her, seduced her, married her, and proven her so wrong. He's not sure he can prove it again this time.

"You can have the house," she says. "You can have everything. I don't need the money you made when you were taking advantage of all those sad strangers. And I don't need you to support me, so don't offer. That would keep us connected, and I just need it to be over. I make enough on my own for what I need."

She stands up and sighs, dry-eyed. He's supposed to say something. He's *always* got something to say. For the first time, though, he's got nothing.

Amused in a painful sort of way, she says, "You know, all this time, all I've wanted was for you to hurt like I do...but you buried it. And because you did, I buried something too. I buried my love for you. I've buried it so deep I can't find it anymore." Her laugh is a hollow, short thing. "No matter how hard I try, I can't dig it out again. Not that you care."

She looks at him, steady and fearless. There's nothing left to say. No amount of pleading left to do, no difference he could make now. The last straw is too light a phrase. This is the last brick in the wall between John and his wife.

She's beautiful. She's always been beautiful. Her mascara is perfectly unsmudged. Her eyeliner nicely in place. When he'd imagined this, there wasn't a dry eye in the house. Not her, not even him. Yet here they stand. His gorgeous wife, the one who he had chased down, fought for, and caught for himself, is flying away from the golden cage he's put her in. He cares. Oh, he very much cares all of a sudden. But not enough to do anything about it.

Neither of them says goodbye.

As John saunters through the house, he notices that the photographs he's always avoided are gone. He doesn't know if it's a mercy or a very clear statement. One that says he doesn't deserve a reminder.

The song "Leaving on a Jet Plane" sings somberly in his head as he peruses his picture-book house. It's not a home. His bedroom is filled with crisp blankets and pillows too fluffed to look like they've ever been used. It's cold and empty. Gutted. She had planned this, perfectly orchestrated to happen between the hours he went to work, fucked someone new, and walked through the door. She'd been ready. It seems unreal, yet more real than any other moment of his life.

Beth's vanity stands empty. When he opens her drawers, he's met with pale, wooden bottoms. No hairbrushes, no foundation dust, no sign she'd ever been there. He idly wonders if she had someone else, but no. Beth wasn't like that. Even if she had a man of interest, she would have waited. Put him off. Pined. Perhaps this is the moment she'd finally look at that imaginary lover with her pretty, crystal blue eyes and say, "I've left him."

Somehow, the thought of being replaced is the thing that finally makes John break down and sob. And when he starts, he doesn't stop. The tears fall, painful and burning.

He still smells like sex.

And John throws up on his pristine floor.

The Rules

"What the hell are you even doing?" *A* asks him. "You've been standing there for an hour." Or whatever passage of time counts as an hour in this place.

"I like it," John says, shrugging.

"But it hurts." *H* eyes him as if he were an anomaly. "Don't you hurt enough already?"

"At least this is a hurt I can control."

He stands alone on the grate in the center of the altar, his heels and the balls of his feet digging into the rusted metal. Anyone who's spent too long going to the bathroom here knows to keep your feet on the stone and just hover your rear above the painful crisscrosses—John's ass learned its lesson the hard way during the first few days when he'd laid on it—but for some reason, the slats digging into his feet today are soothing. Grounding. Like a kind of mindful body meditation.

"I walked on broken glass once," John tells them. "I always wanted to do the hot coal thing too, but I never had the chance."

"Why would you want to do that?" *A* asks him, jaw unhinging as he lets out a few more open-mouthed coughs.

John looks at him with steel in his expression, followed by a little bit of mischief. "To prove I could. To show myself that, even though I was afraid, I could do it anyway."

The sentiment hits the other men hard, John can see it in their faces. Taking action in the face of futility. Controlling what you can control. Maybe he should proselytize to a new group of sheep; a congregation of two is better than nothing.

"Why do it here though?" *H* follows up, obviously thinking that John should be focused on other things.

"Because I can. Because I want to." John's jaw clenches and he looks up, knowing The Bitch is due any minute now. "Because she's not telling me to. Because I have a choice. For once, she's not doing it to me. *I'm* doing it to me. And that matters."

H laughs. "Broken glass. Hot coals. So, you're a masochist then?"

John snorts. "The glass doesn't hurt. They psych you up but it's a sham. I wanted to get a cut or a scar or something to prove I did it, to show off later, but I didn't even feel a thing. I'm guessing they use fake stuff to make sure they don't get sued." Which is a fair business decision, he'd say. Turning to his co-captives, a smile spreads across John's face as he drops his voice low, like a movie bad guy. "Wanna play a game?"

The wet splutter *A* lets out before his laugh is endearing. "That sounds ominous."

"Have you ever played Foot Push?"

They look at him like he has three heads.

"No, seriously, it's easy." John drops on his rear and scoots over to *A,* who seems the least hostile of the two. Bracing on his arms and flexing his healing shoulder blades, John puts his two legs in the air and waggles his toes. "Put your feet on mine."

"You want me to do what now?" *A* asks, eyes narrowed and brows to his hairline.

John's smirk is unending. "Put. Your feet. On mine. I'm bored. I need something to do. My mind's gonna go numb if I don't keep busy."

Running his fingers through the tendrils of his grubby dreads, *A* snorts back a loogie and spits it into what he's deemed "the snot slick stone." Full of colorful truths, that one. Sighing in agreement and therefore giving up his right to complain, the man leans his back against the wall, braces himself, and lifts his feet up.

John can already tell this is a bad idea from the way *A*'s muscles tremble and the man's feet have trouble reaching his own. To help rectify the situation, John keeps his feet at a 90-degree angle and puts them sole to sole with *A*'s, steadying their heels together.

"Now, push me," he says with a grin.

"Go fuck yourself." *H* sneers. "What? You think he's gonna win against you?"

"Oh no, my friend," John eases. "It's not about winning. It's about prolonging the loss." He winks at *A* and the man smiles back at him, shaking his head.

"I can feel the damn indents on your feet," he says.

"Good. So your nerve endings still work. Point in your favor. Now, are you gonna push or am I gonna stuff your ankles into your ears?"

A's thick lips smoosh into each other as he *pfffffts* a raspberry in John's direction. The weight of *A*'s press is so light it's concerning, but John keeps any sign of it off his face. He pretends he's playing with kids. After all, they're not strong either, but that doesn't mean they don't want to try. It's something to do anyway. After he's done with *A*, maybe *H*'s competitive side will kick in and he'll get another round before boredom comes back to bite them. Or exhaustion, more likely.

The first thing John does is let his knees pull back so *A* can follow, gently paddling their feet in small circles until *A* gets a feel for it and starts guiding their motions on his own. Without warning, the frail man pushes hard with a kind of "yah!" sound, and the two men's legs bow wide in a split, making John crack up with a grin.

"Okay, so that's doing it wrong," he chuckles.

"Shut up," *A* gripes through his amusement.

John brings their feet back together and guides them back and forth again. "Use those stringy thigh muscles of yours and hold them together. Pretend you're a virgin trying to protect your special spot."

"You're disgusting," *H* hisses.

"What?" John says. "You think you can do better? I'll take you anytime."

When *H*'s lips purse, John knows he's getting another opponent lined up for the day, and the thought makes him giddy.

With a little shove, *A*'s ankles hover over his chest and he grunts.

"You're a bastard, you know that?"

John's grin couldn't get any wider if it tried. "I may have been told that on occasion."

The other man only scoffs, lips quirked to the side before he grunts and gives a shove, pushing their feet back into neutral position.

"Good show, old man."

"Fuck off," *A* says, but he's giggling this time. It makes him cough a bit, but every hacking expulsion pushes John harder, and he lets his knees go far back over his belly before rushing one leg forward and earning a sharp curse from his gangly competitor.

"What are you doing?" comes a shrill voice from up top.

John's eyes snap up and he actively keeps his face from souring. *A* coughs out his nerves, tucking his face into the crook of his elbow this time.

"Hey, gorgeous." *H* turns on his best smile for her. "Apparently we're playing a ga—"

"*Stop that!*" she hisses. *A* pulls away as if he's been burned. "You're going to hurt them," she scolds John, waggling a finger at him and narrowing a single eye into a weird squint. John doesn't know if she's real-mad or play-mad, or whether one will become the other on the turn of a dime. He lowers his feet like a good boy and backs away, muttering an apology that may or may not sound sincere.

"If you hurt them..." She trails off, fury plain on her face. It's disgustingly strange that she seems to care. "They are mine, not yours!" Ahh, that makes sense then.

Yours to hurt? To starve? John wants to say, but keeps his mouth very shut.

Cujo doesn't seem to be here today, so at least there's that. John hopes it's dead. One less thing to worry about.

She dips out of view for a second and then grunts, pulling up a second bucket to go with the first she left down there.

"I thought"—she huffs out her exertion—"you might need more"—huff, puff—"water."

"Bayyyyby girl!" *H* stands, arms held up. It looks like he's preparing to hug her tight, if only she was closer. "Thank you so much!"

And damned if she doesn't smile the sweetest smile and blush. "I like it when you call me that."

"And I like to call you that," *H* returns.

Discomfort tingles through John's sensibilities and he struggles to keep his face neutral. "Thank you," he says, as nice as he can.

She's looping the ropes around again. "John, get this, will you?"

He stands and lowers *H*'s arms with kindness, tut-tutting him away, though all he gets is a glare in return. He holds his hands up to receive the descending decadence and says again, more earnestly this time, "Thank you." Swallowing, he then decides to play along. "You look pretty today."

Something like love comes over her face as the pail lands between his fingers, the cool condensation something he has to actively try not to lick.

"You say that to everyone." She waves at him like a schoolgirl.

"Only the people who deserve it."

And it earns him a deeper blush, though it fades into a scowl. "Too bad so *many* people deserved it in your life. Did your wife deserve it?"

And now he's out of his depth. He has no idea what to say. All he knows is that everything has suddenly gone very wrong. "What are you talking about?"

She tugs hard and the bucket starts its path back up, slipping from John's hands.

"Wait," ekes out of his throat as his fingertips slip from the plastic, leaving greasy fingerprints.

"You haven't taught him the rules," she growls to the other men.

A stands and looks up at her in supplication. "I'm sorry, love, you didn't tell us to, and we were just being good. He's only at level two trust, like you said. Maybe level three…"

"*Of course* he's level three! If you can live down here and be *friends* that *touch,* you might be even more than that!"

John's mind reels. They say he's level five, but *H* hates it, fights it, so is he really? John doesn't even know what the levels mean. Is level three bad? Is level five good or dangerous?

"I'm sorry," he calls out. "I didn't know we weren't supposed to touch each other!"

"That's not the rule!" she throws back at him, teeth fixed in a sneer as she grabs the pail and hauls it back over the lip of the well.

"Can I know the rules?" he cries. "Please? I don't want to...I don't want to be bad!"

That gives her pause. All three men have their eyes locked on her, and John is worrying his hands together. One of her eyebrows quirks slightly. The sun is shining on her just-so, making her average face clear in the daylight. She hums in thought, tapping her finger against her cheek. "Whether you want to be or not, you are. You've ruined everything you ever had. I know. I met your wife, and she is a sad, sad lady with a sad, sad life."

What?

John's anger comes back, filling him with a whirlwind of vitriol. His mind spins down corridors made of spiderwebs. What does she have to do with his wife?

You bitch. Ohhhh, you horrible bitch.

"If you wanted to be sorry, you should have been sorry to her."

Defensive, he seethes. "What's it to you? I thought you only took *adulterers*. She left me before I even met you!" A truth that has lived on the tip of his dry tongue ever since he found out what the scabbed-over 'A' on his chest means.

H whirls on him, but John continues his death-stare.

She coos. "You think so? Ohhh, you don't even know, do you? Of course, you wouldn't. Too wrapped up in yourself to notice that I'd been following you. Venue after venue, show after show, performance after performance."

An intense feeling of violation laces over his fury. "You did *what?*"

"Sometimes I wore a red wig, sometimes black. Sometimes I'd lose a few pounds, sometimes I'd gain them."

How long? How fucking long? his brain screams.

"You always seemed to like me best in red. I wondered why...until I met your wife."

John wants to kill her.

"Tell me she's okay," he all but screams.

"Like you care," she scoffs.

"I will *always* care!"

"Apparently not enough to stop sleeping with me."

His muscles clench in rage. He wants to climb this cavern of rock and strangle her.

"I always wondered why you never recognized me. I waited for you to figure it out. I had different name tags and different makeup, but I was still me. Then I realized, you never really looked at my face. You never really listened to me. You were too focused on teaching me, I guess."

He's going crazy. He's fucking going crazy.

"You *cunt.*" The filthiest word in his extensive vocabulary, and he throws it at her like a javelin. When she flinches, he knows he hit his mark.

H slaps at him, trying to shove him but getting nowhere. *A* tries to press a hand over his mouth, but it's easy enough for John to slip from his grip.

"You absolute *filthy CUNT!*" He's screaming now, thrashing a bit to push the flailing arms of his co-captives off him. Every wounded look in her eyes is a medal to hang around his neck. He twists to the side to loosen a random hand from his mouth, not knowing who did it and not caring either way. "It's too bad I didn't look at your face. Because if I *did,* I never would have FUCKING *TOUCHED YOU!*"

H dives to the outer circle of the wall and picks up his blunted knife, brandishing it in the light. The soft white stone shines all too brightly in this abysmal place. John freezes then.

A's hand finally successfully latches over his mouth and the other one goes in his hair, yanking his head back, offering his throat to *H*. The man looks poised to do it, and John remembers that he can break them.

The Bitch seems to know it too.

And she wants to protect her pets.

"Stop," she says again. It comes out bland. Mild and disinterested. True to form, she even looks at her nails as if bored. Both men stand down immediately and John is left without a bruise on him, but the hate he sees in their eyes hurts his heart. She scoffs, her rumble nasal and breathy. "If you have that much energy, perhaps you don't need supplies after all."

A lets out a defeated sound and wheezes, holding in another cough. Both men seem afraid to move.

"You have my permission to tell him the rules. All of them." The Bitch stares at John coldly. "You don't seem to appreciate your situation enough to show respect." A grin coils on her face like a writhing snake. "And naughty boys who disobey don't get their supper."

Hearing *H*'s pained sigh and *A*'s small sob snaps something in him. Something else. Something worse.

"IF I EVER GET OUT OF HERE, I'LL KILL YOU, YOU BITCH!"

"Promises, promises." She smirks.

Incoherent, John keeps yelling. Screaming. Real words, nonsense words, cusses, threats. His throat goes raw, and he doesn't care. *A* huddles in his own arms and weeps openly while *H* stares at The Bitch with an expression that apologizes more than anything else. She doesn't look at John and the spittle flying from his mouth, she only stares meanly at *H*.

Over the sound of John's temper tantrum, she says, "Teach him. Because if you don't, you're going to lose your friend. And maybe more."

H nods, just once. He doesn't have to be told again.

John's voice cracks and breaks. He clenches his fist at the sky, impotent and useless. More trouble than he's worth. For all he knows, he's doomed them. His only friends. The only thing keeping him sane in this dungeon. The ones he's hanging his hopes and dreams on as he fantasizes about saving them. This moment is the opposite of saving them.

He bursts into tears, but it doesn't matter. Not one little bit.

———

The night has come on mindlessly, not caring about all the sorrow and agony that goes on below its purple-blue canopy. The stars are out tonight, and John can see the Milky Way again. That means they're far away from city lights. Far away from civilization. Yet another problem to add to the list.

There's little time to think about that. School is in session.

"We are untouchable." *H* looks down at John like he's trash, a scowl so harshly carved into his face, it pulls the hollows of his cheeks into a ghastly expression. His lungs heave in fury, his jutting ribs sliding under the skin in a sickening rhythm as he paces. "That is one of the most deeply rooted rules."

John wants to talk, but he's unable. Instead, he huddles over himself, looking up. Tears still stand in his eyes, his lids burning from the unexpected moisture. He'd been screamed at, slapped at, and guilted to hell and back, and he deserved every moment of it.

"She can hurt us, but you can't. Not now, not ever. None of you newcomers are allowed. He and I, we're special." *H* flicks his chin in the direction of *A*, whose palms are dug so hard into his eyes, John aches to see it. The man's shoulders shudder, his rage dissipated. He looks hollow and wrung out instead.

H points at John roughly, scolding the captured sinner. "You must be gracious, you must be loving, but you have to earn her trust before she'll believe it. You do that by accepting that you failed in your life before now. You need to take responsibility."

Confused, John shakes his head. His voice comes out like a ragged whisper. "How?"

"Admit it," *A* manages to say. "Own it. Be sorry for it."

"Does she have my wife?" John crumbles. Not his ex-wife. In this moment, she is and always was his.

"No." *A* shakes his head, snuffing back wetness. "And she's not involved with her either. That's not what this is about. She likely marked her just to make sure you were a real target. Think what you want about her, know what you do about her, feel what you can't help but feel, but you need to understand that she identifies with every one of the women she's punishing you for."

"What am I supposed to do? Just say, 'Sorry?'"

"You take it." *A* looks at him with swollen eyes John can barely see in the dim light. "Whatever she gives you or chooses not to give you, you take it. You're sorry every day. Every day you look at her, you need to know that she's the only reason you're alive. And if she wants to hurt you, you just let it happen. You make it happen."

"No." John shakes his head. "No, I can't do that."

H leans in and tugs John's hair again, lifting his face into his putrid breath. "You better learn. Make no mistake, if she can take it away, she *will* take it away. And she'll do it as much as she wants until she thinks you're sorry enough."

"No raising your voice," *A* says. "No insults. Be nice."

"No pushing, shoving, or cutting in line," John adds,

bitterly. Children's rules. "Everyone keeps their hands to themselves."

"No." *H* shakes his head, hunkering down to glare at him. "No, that's never been a rule. Especially not for newbies. She makes some of you kill each other. She likes to watch."

John's jaw drops as he imagines it. A real-life *Hunger Games*. He wouldn't put it past her. That sadistic, mind-fucking bitch.

"And we have to watch," *A* says. It's high-pitched and distant. Like he's a lost little boy.

Growling, *H* cuts in, "And sometimes we have to help. Understand?"

John nods, his stomach sick. His guts feel rotted inside.

Rallying, he takes a sniveling breath and confirms, "So, I can't hurt you. I can't even do anything that *looks* like I might hurt you. No matter what, I take her punishments without complaint because I deserve it. I have to play nice, even if she's ready to kill me. If she says jump," he grits his teeth, "I say how fucking high. What else?"

H gestures up. "You don't ask for things. You don't barter. He and I can...barely. But we have to give something up in return. We saved you, got what you needed, and it cost us vitamins. You get any of those yet?"

John shakes his head.

"Exactly. And we don't know when we're getting them back. *If* we're getting them back. You think meat and bread give us enough calcium or potassium or whatever? How long do you think our bodies will last like this? Do you think she'll even remember that we need them? Maybe, but maybe only when it's too late to matter."

"Fine. I hear you." Biting his lips to the point of pain, John holds back a sudden wave of depression. "What else?"

H's voice darkens. "Don't go off script. And that's not her rule, it's mine. If I want you dead, if *he* wants you dead, all we have to do is piss you off enough and let you dig your own grave."

"You don't go further off script than escaping," John challenges. He narrows his eyes at *H*. "You can't kill me. You need me."

"Maybe," the man admits. Opening his arms wide, he chuckles. "Or maybe I just give up."

There is a moment of such heavy silence, John can't take it. Lump in his throat or no, he has to fill the void.

"What are the levels?" John looks at one man, then the other. *H* seems to be done talking to him and just goes across to the other end of the 'Bowl, sitting down, throwing his legs out in a straight line and sighing, obviously exhausted. *A* meets his eyes for a second before flicking them down again and answering.

"Level one: I won't kill you unless provoked. You were level one as soon as we started nursing you. Undid your mouth. Got you your meds." *A* coughs, likely needing some of his own. "Level two: I believe *you* won't kill *me* unless provoked. You hit that when we let your hands go and she scared us into opening your eyes. Level three: I will tell you things. Superficial things, but things. You earned that on your own. It wasn't a gift. It wasn't a necessity. It's just how it happened. It makes it harder and harder to think about you dying. Some made it to level two, but never level three."

John runs his hands through his hair, tugging it until his scalp aches.

"Level four. You never actually hit level four. You skipped it. It's supposed to be: I will tell you my secrets...but you don't tell us secrets, do you? Even though level five is: We trust you with our secrets."

"What secrets?" he hisses.

"You know we were here first. You know the tiniest bit of what we've seen. What we've done. You know we want out, and you know it's the only reason we wanted a 'friend.' We tricked her, and tricking her is deadly."

John nods for a bit, scraping his fingers over the nape of his neck in the silence and thinking the conversation is over, the numbers complete, until *H* goes on in *A*'s place. He sounds both dissociated and passionate. A dangerous, unnerving sort of cocktail.

"Level six: You are mine, whatever that means to me. Friendship, lovers, doesn't matter. All that matters is that I own you. Forever."

The sentiment is more than unhealthy.

"Level seven: I won't kill you, even if you provoke me. No matter how hard you *try* to provoke me. Level eight: I will die for you. Whether I mean to or not. Level nine: I will live for you. Even if I don't want to. Level ten: I will go through hell for you." *H* smiles, lost in his own thoughts.

Afraid to ask, but never knowing when to shut up, John presses, "You two, what level are you at with each other?"

Without hesitation, both reply, "Five," in perfect unison.

Meaning, they are absolutely willing to kill each other if need be...just like they are willing to kill him.

"And her? What's your level with her?"

H is the only one who speaks this time, looking at him with a defeated smirk. "Ten."

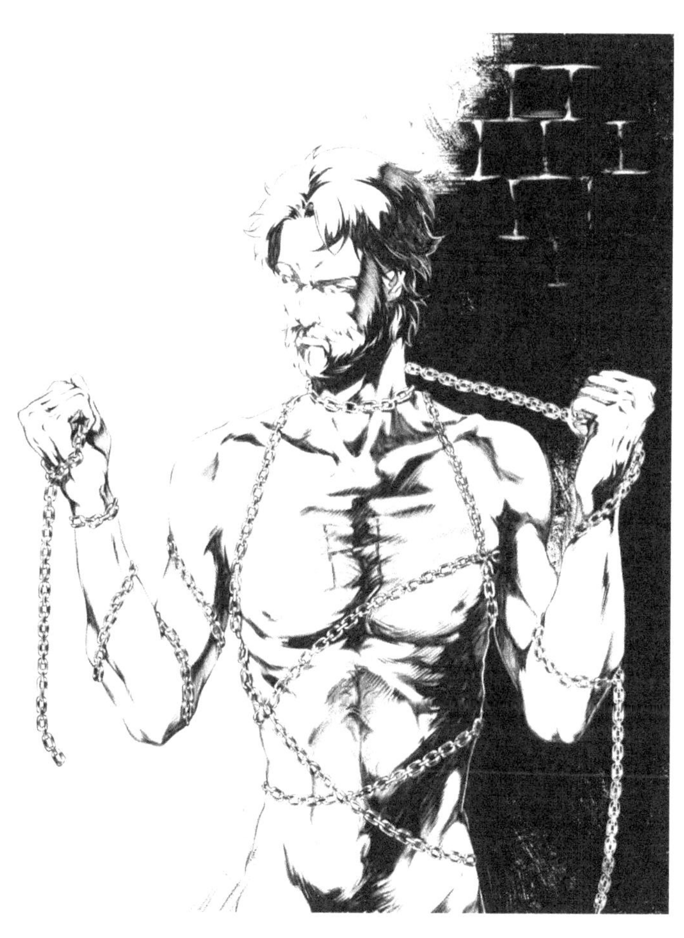

THE PAST -
INTERLUDE FIVE

"*Radical Acceptance*!" John lets the phrase hang heavy in the air, holding two fingers up and waving them around slightly, drawing his audience's enraptured eyes. He repeats, staccato and clipped, "Radical. Acceptance."

These are just a few of the magic words he needs to drill into their minds. He's weaved them into his presentation at least ten times to ensure that, if they walk away with nothing else, this one concept will be branded into their hollow heads.

"Things have happened in your life. Some of them you couldn't control. They were inflicted upon you by God or the world or horrible, terrible, loathsome people. Some you even inflicted upon yourself. You may have asked for those terrible situations by name, or you may have called them to you the same way candy calls to children...too sweet and vulnerable to be passed up, but unable to help it. Not your fault, but your fault anyway. Still, it doesn't really matter how your pain was born. Your hopelessness. Your sorrow. What *really* matters...is what you do with it.

"Radical! Acceptance!" John says again, punctuating each word with his rising fingers. "You can't change what happened, no matter how much you may want to. There is no eraser. There are no *take-backsies* or *do-overs*. With radical acceptance, you understand that concrete concept all the way to your bones. And it's only then that it will finally hit home… that *you can't change it.* The past is the past. And it's immutable.

"That's when the magic happens, ladies and gentlemen. Think about how much time you spend, day in and day out, ruminating on your past. Weeping over the cards life has dealt you. Reliving those moments over and over, wishing they were something other than what they truly were. It's like your body doesn't want to forget those moments. Forgive those moments. It's carved into your brain like looming statues. And that's why the word *radical* comes into play."

The audience is made up of wide eyes, their minds in exaltation as they stare at him. John always wants the house lights up a bit so he can see their faces. It's what gives him energy. It's what gives him life. This endless feedback loop of their need for him and his need to be needed.

Look at me. That's right. Feel this.

"Radical means many things," John says, and because none of them have memorized the dictionary the way he has, he elucidates. "One is: a person who advocates for complete reform. And *acceptance* is allowing yourself to receive or undertake something that is offered to you. My friends, I am offering you the chance to *reform.* To *accept.* To *overcome.*

"I'm not just talking about the inky black demons of your past. Those are already written in the book of Your Life. I'm talking about the *future* demons that will stain your tomorrows as the pages turn. The ones that ruined you yesterday *and* the ones that will ruin you in the months and years to come. Poison you. Let me ask you this, how many of you are poisoned with demons?"

John raises his hand because it's the God's honest truth.

More hands go up, shyly at first, but as the number that reaches for the vaulted ceiling grows, more are able to admit their flaws. They are together in their misery.

"And how many of you think you can make those demons go away?"

So many hands drop, but John's stays up. This is the most important lie he sells them during each and every conference performance. It's job security. In truth, these people don't need John. They need therapists and uppers and someone to love them. But here they are, listening and begging to belong. For someone to care. And oddly enough, John does care in a way. He cares about the sheer number of them. So, he makes them believe they have nothing to gain from any of those other charlatans. He's the pusher of the only drug they need to buy. Him.

"If your hand went down, my friends, it just means you and I need to spend more time together—and while I do offer one on one sessions, that's not what tonight is about." The microphone near his mouth neither hisses nor pops, truly good quality, and the wireframe that wraps it around his ear is comfortable for once as well. He opens his hands up wide. "I still have demons. I create new ones too, from time to time. But you know what else I do?"

Some move up to the edge of their seats.

"I kill my old ones. *That's* what I do. I look at them first though. See all their nooks and crannies, their pits and cracks, their dirt and their disease. And then I accept them, no matter how much I hate them. I *name* them. I say, 'Hello, you shmuck. I see you trying to make this bad thing happen to me today'...but like other toxic things in my life, I decide not to engage. I decide not to even say schmuck's name anymore... because he doesn't deserve my attention. I don't even need to *look* at him. And then, after a while, sometimes a long while, he shrivels up...and then he dies.

"That's the most crucial part. After you *accept* he exists, you have to *act* in order to slay your demons. You have to do something different. There are a million ways to get something wrong, but only a finite way to get things right. *Accept and Act!*"

Another concept he needs them to walk out of here with. After all, that's what his books are named. A little marketing trick to make them foam at the mouth. To say, "But, John, how can lowly little me *Radically Accept*? How do I *Accept and Act*?" and the retail person just outside the door happily replies, "Well, here are some signed copies of the books that will teach you. That will be $49.95. Oh? A limited recording from his website? That will be another twenty dollars. Twenty-*five* if you want access to the audiobooks, all read by John himself."

He takes a deep breath. This is the part he hates himself for a little bit, though it has to be done. He does it to shove a spike under the fingernails of their self-esteem. If they feel low enough, then they'll crave the little John-made adrenaline high that comes at the end of his act. He'll leave them cheering in a mindless euphoria that will last exactly twenty minutes. Enough time for them to open their wallets, and enough time for him to slip away.

"If you don't *accept* and *ACT*—that last word being the most important—you wallow in your sorrow, don't you? Lying on your couch and crying."

You know, like every sad person ever.

"But isn't sloth one of the seven deadly sins, my friends?"

Not that John believes in religion one bit.

"And if you do it with a bag of Doritos in your hand, well, now you're a glutton too, aren't you? And then you're left alone in the dark with crusty, orange fingers, binging season 57 of the latest trash, avoiding what you could be."

He pauses for effect.

"Me. You could be *me*. On stage, owning your pain and being alive. Overcoming!"

He sells himself like a product. And they're allllllll buying.

"You know my tragedy. I've shared it with you. Some of you have wept for me—and I appreciate that, I truly do—but I'm done weeping for me. Done. I've been able to move beyond it, and you can move beyond it too. You and I are no different."

Which is bullshit. He's up here and they're down there. And, for better or for worse, they will *always* be down there. Glassy eyed with a veritable library full of books at their disposal containing answers they don't read, though they love to pretend they do. During conversations, they pepper in little quotes from that one single, solitary chapter they read before their TV called to them. Success sits on a shelf while they all die inside. He'd say he pities them, except that he loves them so very much for exactly what they are.

Faceless. Nameless.

And needy.

———

John mills about after the show—the *speech*—and decides to check out the conference sales floor for a bit. It's larger this time. His venues get bigger and bigger, as do his speaking fees. Still, he's not ready to sequester himself to the castle of his car, driving home and listening to whatever repetitive be-bop is streaming. Instead, he waits to be recognized by all the people who attended his keynote so he can chat with them. Lay on the charm. Song and dance a little. Get his teeth into them.

The better to eat you with, my dear.

He is on the prowl. After tonight's high, he's not ready to

go home to his wife. Every time he looks at her, all he sees is sadness, and he doesn't want to live that life. He doesn't want to be that depressed, self-isolated person. That is why he walks the floor, looking to seduce someone. It's not hard. He's what they want to be, after all, and if he deigns to look at them, they imagine they can replace the pretty wife he told them went to heaven while slides of her image had played behind him on stage. They see his wedding ring and want to be the woman who makes him want to take it off. Replace it with a new one. Both pretty and not so pretty girls with starry eyes look at him like a rock god just because he stands on a platform where lights hit him from every angle. They want to be a balm on the pain he's already buried.

So he fucks them. And he fucks them, and he fucks them to tell himself it doesn't hurt, so that when he looks at his wife, he can pretend that it's true. He can try to be strong for her instead of just avoiding her. She's sad enough as it is, and he can keep his secrets quite well. He drowns his sorrows in sex the way that alcoholics drown their livers in poison, but at least this is good exercise.

That's where his mind is when a woman with red hair, red nails, and a pretty laugh approaches him. They like it when he looks off into space like he's thinking. It's like an invitation.

The sound of the hustles and bustles continue around him without pause, people selling their wares and witchcraft. Their knowledge and knickknacks. Their excellence and their education. To her though, this giggling newcomer, the situation has narrowed down to just one thing. Him. He has her already and he hasn't even opened his mouth yet. He doesn't ask her name, but she'll be screaming his soon enough.

Death, Then
And Now

John is using the one bucket she'd left them with, the second having literally slipped through his fingers. The tiny bit of water they'd managed to get into this plastic, yellow monstrosity is completely clouded with mud at this point, but John's unwilling to sully any more of their drinking water in order to replace it.

It's raining a little tonight, cold for the first time, and John is quivering. Even so, he'd mustered the strength to drag their dirty trough to the edges of the altar, letting it catch the rain. The bucket went immediately under the drip-drip-droplets as well while the other men stood facing the sky with their mouths open. It's a lightning strike image, one that burns itself into John's retinas. They're like guppies. Skinny, bony little fish om-noming at the clouds as if skimming for imaginary food.

The worst part is when John joins them.

A stops for a bit to cough and hock out something stringy, but then he goes right back at it. John doesn't want to blame himself for *A*'s illness, so he blames the trough instead. It's the moss, he figures. Moss shouldn't be toxic or anything, but in

John's mind it might as well be carrying the plague. He and *H* drink out of it and are doing just fine, so he imagines *A*'s immune system must be on the fritz. Who could blame it?

When the rain stops, they curl onto themselves and shiver. Through John's grit teeth, he says, "We need to hold each other."

H meets his eyes with a haughty lift of one wet eyebrow.

"No, I'm serious. We need to share our body heat."

Shaking his head, *A's* muscles flutter under his thin skin, his roadmap of veins bulging. "I don't wanna give you whatever this is." He gestures from his chest to his head in frustration. "We just fixed you."

"Your throat sore?" John asks, guilt welling up.

"Doesn't matter," is what comes back, *A* all-out trembling now.

"Can she get us more meds?"

He's met with *H*'s dark laugh. "We haven't even gotten *food* yet. You think she's going to gift us with anything special?"

John's teeth chatter as he wraps his arms tighter around his knees, changing the subject. "I've got the third rock out, working on the fourth after she leaves today. That's the last one. After that, all that's left is to dig our way up and out."

John's been going wide instead of deep, and there are a couple reasons why. Number one is that he needs to be able to fit his entire body into that precious escape tunnel, preferably without getting stuck and choking on the no doubt flavorful mud until he suffocates to death. Number two is that, once he's ready to dig deep, he'll finally have to put his shoulders in. Then his chest. Then his waist. At that point, there is no hiding what he's doing anymore. She's not stupid, and clumps of mud in his hair would be a red flag if there ever was one. It's something he won't be able to hide, no matter how deep into the shadows of the 'Bowl he skulks.

"If I can get us out of here and into the yard, I know we can sneak away and find a town somewhere. Or if there's another house nearby, we can go there. As long as there's a person, there's a phone. Help. Hospitals. Police. We're out in the boonies here, I know, but *something* has got to be close. If I can get us out, you'll get everything you need." He nods at *A*. Over and over again, he nods. "We can do this, I promise. It'll be alright. You'll be fine."

"I'll believe it when I see it," *H* says, grimacing as he tugs at his beard, wringing the damp out into the palm of one hand before licking it. "There are too many *ifs* in your little spiel for my liking."

"Before, we didn't even have *ifs*. We had expiration dates," *A* reminds, his voice hoarse. He looks like he'll say more but doesn't bother in the end. Instead, they fall into one of their long-lasting silences.

John shudders from the chill. He can't sleep like this. He waits for the sun to hurry up and poke its head over the horizon—warm him up and dry him off. It's not cold enough for his breath to plume, but it's cold enough to suck. Trying to keep his mind off it, he babbles. "You guys said I never shared a secret, right? Well, I've got one for you."

Both look at him in interest, as urgent to stop the boredom as they are the chill.

"I was a motivational speaker before all this." John points a finger in a swivel.

It's *H* that laughs at him, steepling his stick-like fingers over his brow and shutting his eyes. His shoulders heave with chuckles. "Of course you were."

A snorts. "That explains a lot. Not really a secret though. That's pretty level three."

John grumps. "It's not like I know what *you* used to be before all this."

"Iron works," *H* says. "I used to make handmade crap for

rich people. Banisters and art. Ornamental gates and custom gazebos. Stuff like that."

John whistles. "That sounds like you can make a pretty penny."

H shrugs, staring off into the distance. "When you can get the jobs, anyway. People don't usually need more than one steampunk sculpture in their rose garden. Too bad, so sad."

Coughing, *A* idly starts to braid his dreadlocks into chunks of frizzled black. "I was a teacher. Eleventh grade English." He shrugs. "I liked that age. Teenagers are fine, it's the tweenagers who are the assholes. I blame puberty."

John has to laugh at that.

"Did you used to travel or…?" *A*'s eyes glitter and *H* looks at John like he's hungry for stories.

"Not too far, no. Even though I was doing…what I was doing…I knew my wife needed me close by, you know?"

"What's a job like that even like?" *H* asks, scooting a little closer. It makes John perk up and smile. It's nice to get the man's guard down.

"It's one part actor and one part screenwriter-who-plagia-rizes," John says. "You tell the same story with perfect, believable tears twice a day while cobbling together cool phrases from people way smarter than you. Build an appendix to keep from getting sued and boom! Money. Selling people solutions to problems they made all by themselves."

His co-captives both snicker at him before shuddering a bit more, molars clicking together as their moist skin throws their heat away.

"That's pretty cynical," *A* says.

John shrugs with his lips pressed together as if to say, "What can you do?" He scrubs his scruffy chin against his knees, feeling their lengthening prickles scratch his magic itchy spot as he contemplates. "There is a secret hidden in there though. Other than the punishable obvious." He scoffs but doesn't meet their eyes this time. "One day, my wife decided to come see one of my speeches. It was close enough to home, and she wanted to watch me 'razzle-dazzle the crowd.' Her words, not mine." There's a longing sort of sweetness in his stupid grin. It fades quickly.

"She'd been depressed for a while. She mellowed out eventually—time heals all wounds, after all—but back then, she was really bad off. Would go days without talking. When I said she could come, it was the first time she'd smiled in weeks. It was small, but it was there. She kept saying she was excited to see me 'in all my glory.'" He does air quotes around the phrase, his softness turning sarcastic and condescending.

"Honestly, it pissed me off. I used to...well...I used to *exaggerate* during my engagements, so to speak. When she came, I had to cut out my whole heart-wrenching routine about how I mourned my wife when she died horribly in a tragic accident. The story, the slides, the slogans. It shortened my presentation by ten minutes. I was furious, but I couldn't show it. I didn't want her to know I was using her as a gimmick. I also didn't want her to see how fake I was. Or was becoming, I don't know."

He nudges his fingers against his letter, breathing in and out, trying to settle the heartache the memory brings. "From then on, I made sure I had to travel two hours or more to get to venues. Close enough to home that I didn't have to fly, but far enough away that she wouldn't ask to come. It was more than fine with her. It upset her to be in the audience. There were some tragedies I couldn't cut out of my story, and she couldn't bear to relive them."

John winces. He hadn't meant to say that.

There is a beat of silence before *A* asks the inevitable. "What tragedies?"

But no. We're not going there tonight. Maybe not ever. "I don't want to talk about it."

H groans theatrically. "It was just getting good!"

"Glad my misery amuses you," John mutters.

"What else is it supposed to do?" the man says with a smirk. "Inspire interpretive dance?"

John sighs through his nose, irritated and indignant, reminding himself to never share anything ever again. He sulks in silence, closing his eyes and trying to drift off as the sky turns to the beginnings of a buttery yellow and the temperature starts to rise.

After a few wet hacks and snuffles, *A* says, "Hey." It comes out quiet. Soft. Miserable.

"Hey what?" *H* asks.

"Hey, I'm really sick," he admits.

John gets on his hands and knees and crawls over, putting a palm to his forehead. It's hot. Not burning, not yet anyway, but hot. John fingers *A*'s throat near his pulse and feels the swollen lymph nodes, making him grunt with pain. The man coughs a little more and swallows it.

Shit. There's no lying to himself anymore. "I think he has what I did." John looks at *H* with fear in his eyes. "You can't get anything for him?"

The man grimaces. "I won't ask now. We're not in a position to get any favors. If I do it too early or if I lay it on too thick, I'll lose trust." He looks at *A* with a meaningful expression, holding their gazes together for a heated minute. "And I'm *not* gonna lose trust."

A nods, some unspoken understanding passing between them before he breaks down into a fever-tremble.

"My trust doesn't exist yet," John looks at them, whispering, "so I can't lose anything. Maybe I can—"

"Dig," *H* cuts him off. "If you've got another stone to get, you get it. If you've got more mud to move, then move it. Seems you're our only hope, Obi-Wan Kenobi."

A huffs a little, pained laugh. "I liked those movies."

"I did too," John says with a tiny smile.

"Cheesy seventies trash." *H* snorts. "But I'd watch it anyway. I liked the bad guy's helmet."

———

The Bitch leans on the edge of the Fishbowl, humming like Snow White at the most twisted wishing well possible. All she needs is the tweety birds and the poison apple. Instead, all she has is the panting mutt. German Shepherd? No, probably not big enough to be that.

H stands alongside John, gazing up. It's hard to see her face this morning, but her cold fury from the other day seems to have disappeared. For that, John is grateful. He tries to remember what attracted him to her in the first place, but it's not like he was all too discerning. At the bar where she took him, all he can remember is pretty nails and pretty teeth. He'd like to use his nails and teeth on her right now. He'd take her apart the way Cujo does the rabbits.

Watching her in silence, muscles tense and tired, John's fingers flit to the pock marks where his lips had been sewn shut. He's getting dehydrated and can feel the skin flaking off as his face turns to sandpaper. Somehow, he's supposed to prove that he's grateful for this.

"Good morning!" she calls, charming in her brightness. Wonder of wonders, she's brought the bucket again...and the little basket! The basket means food! John's heart is in his throat and his mouth stings with the want to salivate. "Come and help me, John!"

So he does, nudging *H* out of the way and stretching his arms up. When she sees him, she sighs as if disappointed. He clears his throat and says, "I'm helping…" But it's not defensive in the slightest. It's plaintive. Apologetic if anything.

Her sigh morphs into one of pleasure this time. "I know you are." Her voice lightens again. "Did they teach you the rules?"

"Yes." He nods, his hands on the lowering bucket. Does he yank it down like instinct begs, or does he behave like a good boy and not risk losing it for another day? "I understand now, and I…I can talk about what happened with you if you want. What I did."

Her voice drops an octave. "I'm not ready to talk about it."

"Then we won't," he reassures. His chin dips, and he eyes the floor, something like relief, something like disappointment pounding in his mind. He might have been able to build some good will if they talked, or he might have just fucked it up again. He's not sure how sincere he can truly sound at this point.

The bucket is fully in his hands now and *H* is wrestling with the knots to get it undone as fast as possible before she can change her mind. Without having to be told, John dumps it in the trough and starts to tie it back up to be brought to the top.

She hums through a smile. "Thaaaaaank you!" The *you* tweaks up into a lilt at the end. "I've got meat and bread for you all. I think I forgot to bring it the past few days…"

Not that she says, "I'm sorry."

"That's alright, baby girl," *H* tells her, bumping John with the deep ridge of his hip so he can be on the receiving end of the food. "Do you mind if we eat it now, or would you like us to wait until you go?"

"Now is okay."

Once *H* has it in his grasp, John undoes the knots this time, staring at the heap of it. He doesn't know if the meat will help or hurt him at this point. It gave him horrible diarrhea once, and he can't afford to lose that kind of weight or water, but his stomach reminds him that it hates him, so John decides to give in. Calories are calories.

He casts his eyes over to *A* who still sits on the ground, not looking up. He seems more withered than normal, if such a thing was possible, the knobs on his spine fluxing up and down as he breathes, clearing his throat too many times and coughing as quietly as he can. He's too weak for this.

Something has to be done.

Dread. All John feels is dread. But this is his…friend. His level five. If he's not allowed to say it in words, perhaps he can say it in body language. John gets on his knees and touches *A*'s forehead in concern, fingering his throat again.

See it, Bitch. See what he needs and give it to him.

John stands up to take a piece of bread and starts to pull out the soft inside, ducking back down to give it over, but *H* snags his wrist, shaking his head back and forth. John looks up in terror, wondering if he was caught doing something wrong, but she's not even looking. She's whistling mindlessly to the blue of the sky.

Under his breath, *H* hisses, "I am *not* losing trust." He flicks his eyes to the ground. "He is."

A's voice is hoarse and pathetic. He coughs, wet and rumbling, and when she finally looks down at them, he says, "I want to go home."

John's eyes fly wide, and he twists his face skyward to look at her. She seems stunned. The plea seems so wrong. So out of place. So heartbreaking.

So fucking dangerous.

"I want to go home, honey. Please," *A* begs her.

John feels the sudden urge to drop to his knees and shut him up just like they did to him, but *H*'s grip, no matter how feeble, holds him at bay. It's not cold anymore, but John is still trembling.

Dark doesn't describe her voice. "You are home."

A gets up on his haunches, looking to the clouds, seeing her, letting the sun kiss his fevered face. "I'm sick!" he manages to yell, and it sounds like his tonsils are grinding on each other. "I'm *sick,* and I'm *scared,* and I *want to go home!*"

John's words from when he touched down. Verbatim.

A weeps and hunches over, tearing at his hair like a child having a fit. Ice and fire slip up and down John's body, waiting for her reply. There is a cacophonous silence except for dry tears and congestion. John grips the rope laying slack in his hands and fights back the urge to scream. Scream what? He's not sure. But he's afraid. Deeply, chillingly afraid.

He looks at her one more time, and it seems as if she'll say something. Her expression is inscrutable and her end of the rope creaks in her fists. Her lips part. Her mouth drops open.

And outside the well, something screams. A shriek with masculine undertones. Her head spins to the side and the dog goes ballistic. She utters one, horrible word.

"No."

It's not directed at them. It's at the distance. Somewhere they can't see. The shriek becomes a bellow, and it comes and comes. With a wrench, the rope flies up and out of John's hands, but she doesn't bother bringing it up all the way. Still, it's well out of arm's reach when the terror on her face drives her into action.

The dog bolts, it's dog collar ching-ching-ing, and The Bitch takes off along with it. John strains to hear each metallic strike of the dog tags against each other, trying to count the steps that lead away. To a house? To something? How many steps? He can't tell how many steps! Perhaps it was too many to count...

Still, the someone cries out from far, far away.

John whispers, "Will he come down here?"

H looks up at the circle of sunlight. "No. It's too late for that."

———

Any desire John had to play nice is gone. The far-off bellows of the unknown man had become squeals, had become *nothing*. No one in the 'Bowl talks. No one does anything. And because she might come back, John can't dig. He's filled with a tense fury. Terror and anguish and futility churn in his gut, burning through his veins. There's nothing to do but feel this. No distractions. No hiding. No *nothing*. He feels like he's going to break, or break something else.

John grabs the sides of the trough with both hands and takes a slurp to cool his fire. The food is already gone except for *A*'s, and he doesn't seem to want it. The concern makes John's bile rise now that his body has reason to make it again. He's always had a nervous stomach, and this is way beyond nerves.

Who was that man? Another victim, that's all he knows. Another screaming stranger.

John wants to scream too.

He clasps the end of the trough, fighting back the urge to upend it. To smash the rotting wood. To stomp and shout and throw his new friends into the walls. Mash them into bloody patterns until she does something other than ignore them. Let his adrenaline turn him into a rabid ape, a man-beast unable to be blamed for its resistance to captivity.

He eyes the strawmen before him who sit, watching him prowl with a hollow detachment. No one says anything. No one attempts to de-escalate. Perhaps, for that reason alone, John's two co-captives are fools.

If they're untouchable, if they're supposed to outlive everyone else, what will she do if he tries to kill them? If he hurts them bad enough, will she have the compassion—the possessive *urge*—to somehow take them up topside and heal them? The mouth of this dungeon is wide enough to get a person through, John knows that for a fact. After all, he got down here with flying colors, didn't he?

For a moment, he truly contemplates if he can save his co-captives by hurting them. If he can tear them up just enough to get them stitched. Or maybe he should just kill them and get it over with. A mercy for the men who deserve it most.

And that's when she comes back.

The fucking Bitch comes *back*.

What did you do to him? is fighting in the back of John's throat, begging to be let out. *What happened to the man in the distance? Did you let your dog maul him, you cunt? Did you stab him to death? Eat him? What?*

John paces, unable to do much else, and glares up at her. Jerking his head in *A*'s direction, though the man does not thank him for it, John says, "He's sick. Sick like I was. You gonna do anything about it? If you like watching us so much, the least you can do is try to keep your pets alive. More fish in the Fishbowl."

Her frown of exhaustion only incites him further.

"What did you do to that poor bastard, anyway? Why is he so quiet, huh? Is he dead? Passed out? Did you drug him to keep him quiet? Are you going to kill him now or just hurt him? If he's not coming down here, what happens next? How many are you going to take, you vicious bitch?"

H just puts his head in his hands. There's no covering John's mouth now, and he knows it. *A* doesn't look at John either, he just gazes up into the face of his mistress, pleading. It's disgusting.

John snaps his fingers. "Oh, that's right. How could I forget? You want that guy up there to suffer your feminine wrath, don't you? Were you cheated on too, cunt? Is that why you do all this? How very *boring*. How trite and mundane. Just like every fucking serial killer everywhere, aren't you? Can't you at least be more original about it?" John's grin is something that could make children cry. It's unhinged. It's self-righteous. It's ruined.

"You're completely replaceable," she tells him, cold and matter of fact.

He ignores her. "Did you ever think your little game has a shelf-life? You better try a little harder to keep us all alive, *Baby Girl,* because sooner or later you're gonna get too old and ugly to get laid. How are you gonna get guys then? How are you gonna lift them into your car when your forty-five-year-old back goes out, *Sweetheart?*"

"Make him stop," she growls.

"What are they gonna do? Slap me to death? Poke me with sharp rocks? What are *you* gonna do? Starve all of us? I'd like to see you try it."

H's head snaps up and he looks at John like he's betrayed them.

"I'll outlast them both—your precious firsts. They say you always remember your firsts, don't they, *Honey?* Don't they, *DARLING?*" He spreads his hands out wide in welcome, just as stupid and pig-headed as he's ever been, thinking he's invincible when he's very, very mortal and very, *very* flawed. "You wanna hurt me, cunt? Come on then. Hurt me." His damning words are, "I dare you."

And everything falls into silence.

She steps back and away, and John grins. He won't look at the men who stare at him in terror. He won't think about what he's just done. He's going to stay right here, right now, in his moment of triumph. Of satisfaction.

And that's when the blue tarp comes down. It has a crumpling sound that's unmistakable for anything else. Before anyone can react, it falls in a pile over the altar, covering it completely. *H* has enough time to whisper the word "Jesus..." before she opens the hose.

Like a firehose, every blast of it is stinging cold and painful. She aims right at John, knocking him to the ground with the sheer force of the cascade. The pressure is overwhelming, ramming into his chest and face, icicle nails raking across his flesh. He can't stand. He can't breathe. It's pummeling his face, filling his mouth with water, and he can't even cough it out. His lungs burn, his blood vessels pop, and he's choking, he's drowning, he's—

A somehow pulls him to the side, just barely getting John's torso out of the deluge, and he takes a horrible gasp, head spinning as his skin cries. *H* stands on the other side of the well, looking up like he knows what comes next.

The wintery wetness gathers at their feet, the tarp tamped down hard by the waterfall smashing it. John's panic doubles and he leans down, trying to tug the sheet of plastic from the grate. It hurts and he yelps, but he needs to pull it away or the water won't drain. The tiniest bit of crisscross reveals itself, but it's too much to handle. He's too weak. And when he falls back onto his rear, the water goes up to his hips.

The hose changes angle, pinning him to the ground again, and he gasps for air, pulling nothing but frigid into his mouth and lungs, swallowing it. Breathing it.

So much water.

So *fast*.

John manages to scramble under the shelter of the well's lip once more, clinging to *A*'s legs like little lifelines. He cowers and cries out until the rising water hits his armpits and he forces himself to stand. He leans against the wall, head to stone, coughing. He can't get enough air in.

Even standing, it goes thigh high. Hip high. Cold, so cold it's biting. John's breaths come in rasps, too hard, too fast. His head swims and his lips go numb with fear. With terror. Sheer panic. No. A panic *attack.* His chest heaves and he knows right then and there, down to the very bottom of him, *She's going to drown us.*

And his vision whites out.

THE PAST -
INTERLUDE FOUR

The surgeon stands over John, a sympathetic but practiced look on his face. One he's likely given a million times.

An antiseptic smell fills John's nostrils, a bitter sort of clean. Annoying blips and bleeps call out from other rooms to the tune of life. He can't stand them, but he'd give anything, *everything* to hear one of those blip patterns right about now. To see those arcs of green as they measure the beat of a heart, proving that it's strong and working and alive. But it's not. She's not. And neither is her sister.

Alexandra went down eight days ago. He'd counted each hour of each day in a panic, trying to save Amber before it was too late. Yeah, the twins had headaches. Yeah, they were clumsy. Accident prone. Covered in little bruises and scrapes. Stitches sometimes. Yeah, sound was often too loud, or the light was too bright, making them cower with their hands over their ears and their vision tucked away toward the ground to find the soothing darkness. Who knew it was this? That it had always been this.

The other doctor, their regular doctor, the one John wants

to pull apart *piece* by *piece,* had cited "Childhood Migraines" and potential "High-functioning Autism." Nothing that required further testing. Nothing worth an expensive, out of network MRI, certainly. But when Alexandra dropped at school, convulsing, she was already gone before the ambulance came. It was too late. Only then did the pediatrician order that expensive MRI. It took days to get, but once John's second darling was sedated and they put her into that metal tube, they hadn't even finished the imaging before rushing her into emergency surgery.

Watching your child go under anesthesia is one of the most horrifying things in the world, completely antithetical to everything your parental instincts tell you to do. Amber had an IV with tentacled tubes leading to overhead bags, but she took it like a champ as she sat upright on her little bed waiting to go under. John told her how beautiful she was, over and over, petting black hair that was messy and tangled. Beth would have to comb it out later, he knew. At his praise, her little cupid's bow lips tipped up into a smile as she looked at him, held tightly in his arms. It's then that they started pumping her full of whatever needed to go in.

When Amber's eyes fluttered shut and she sagged in John's arms—a sudden, terrifying thing—the nurses flooded around her, urging him out of the way when all his body did was scream to stay. Stay with his *baby.* Because his baby *needed him!* But a gentle nurse hushed him, telling John it was okay as she half-led, half-dragged him from the room, saying it was natural to feel this way. John's eyes welled with tears, and it was all he could do not to break down. Scream. Fight his way back in to snatch his little girl and bring her someplace safe and warm and awake.

Beth was in the waiting room. Her eyes flicked back and forth between both of his, clutching and worrying her hands together, expecting the worst as his tears spilled over. But the blessed nurse told his wife everything was fine. Amber took to the anesthesia *just fine.* But *NOTHING* was fine! Because even if Amber was here, Alex was gone. Her little laugh and her crinkling nose—mirrored perfectly on her sister, but still different—was gone.

It was like John was going to die.

In the end, the tumor pressed on Amber's spinal cord, about 3-inches large, cutting off the necessary fluids and smashing her cerebellum against the back side of her head. That was why she was so clumsy. When they had taken apart her sister, they'd found the exact same. Twins, the same in everything. Even in this.

Her post-surgical stroke was the last thing their second baby ever did. Six years on this earth isn't long enough, not by a long shot. John had failed them, and it was too late to change that eviscerating fact. Too late to do anything. Why didn't he fight for them harder, when it might have still mattered?

It all comes down to fucking insurance. His shit job only paid for the kind where you had to pull goddamned teeth to get anything done, but John never knew that the girls' problem was dangerous enough to *have* to go pull teeth. He would have. God knows he would have. Out-of-network, covered or not, he would have gone into hock for the rest of his life to stop this. Paid out of pocket. Millions. Billions.

He loves his babies forever and ever.

And now they are gone.

———

When John enters the room, Beth is engraving scribbles into their family photo, obliterating the girls' faces with a sharpie and digging in so hard, she's about to tear the paper.

John is holding his stomach, nearly doubled over with his lips quivering as he watches her, unseen. She's making small noises, stifled sobs, as she omits their children from their life.

In truth, they have a million copies of that photo. All the sizes that exist. They gave them to every person who knew their names, but they still had fistfuls left. Still...it's not the picture. It's the premise.

"Why?" is all he can say, broken and small. "Why would you do such a thing?"

"Because they don't exist," she says, not looking at him, snuffing back something wet, her shoulders working as she continues to blacken their beautiful faces in malignant ink. "They may as well have never been here at all!"

Because he can't bear to let her continue that train of thought, he says, "Beth, the table. The ink is going through..." as if that would get her to stop.

She rounds on him then, teeth bared in a sneer, white and straight and ready to rip him apart. Wordlessly, she thrusts what's left of the photo to the floor but keeps the black marker gripped in her hand, turning back to mark the wooden surface of the coffee table directly. She makes lines and curlicues with grunts and snarls. Stretching her whole arm, she gets up on her hands and knees to make sure she gets every angle of the fucking thing.

John doesn't know what to say. He never knows what to say. He's at a loss and he's hurting while his wife is losing her mind. "Please, honey," he begs.

"IT WASN'T ENOUGH!" she screams, turning at an angle and going for the couch now. Pleather and cheap, it accepts the ink like the punishment it's intended to be. *"IT WASN'T ENOUGH!!"* she shrieks, going for the wall now, the end table, anything and everything she can reach.

With all the courage he can muster, he approaches his wife from behind and loops his arms around her waist, digging his nose into her curly red hair. "Please," he says again. "Please, Beth." A whisper. A plea. He's begging. He just can't do this. He can't bear this.

The sound she makes isn't even a wail. She sinks to the carpet, dragging him down with her as she keens. Turning in his arms, she buries herself in his chest, panic-sweating an acrid tang as she sobs. John wants to sob too. John wants to break. John needs his own comfort and to have his moment, but she's taking it all.

And so, John disconnects. He disconnects from his wife; he disconnects from his heart. He can't let himself feel this. Not now, maybe not ever. So he numbs out, stroking her back and offering shushes he doesn't even hear. She trembles, but he can't feel it. His nerves may as well be dead. She sucks in her wracking cries, and John goes cold.

He loves his babies. He loves his wife. But in this moment...?

In this moment, he hates her.

PRECIOUS, PRECIOUS LIFE

Night makes everything worse.

Desperate, the three of them hold each other and shake. Their teeth clack as exhaustion sets in, no one bothering to speak. There's no real point to their silence, but what could they possibly say? "I'm wet," "I'm cold," "What the fuck is wrong with you," and, "Go to hell, you piece-of-shit asshole," had all made their rounds and retired to the silent echoes of repetitive thought.

John can tell she's done this before. You don't have to be a brain surgeon to figure that out. He remembers *H*'s face vividly as the tarp came down. He knew what was going to happen. What was happen*ing*. In the punishment of the past, John wonders how deep the water was. Right now, the frigid wetness crests to the bottom of his ribs. He's nearly convulsing with the cold, yet fatigue makes him want to sink down deeper into it. Panic attacks tend to sap everything from inside you, and the truth of that fact slams John in the face every time he has one. This is no different. There is no reprieve.

He misses his meds. Self-assigned or otherwise. He misses sex. He misses feeling in control. Even in his downward spiral, he was choosing explicitly how he wanted to crash and burn. He was a proud man once, yet look at him now. Perhaps that's why he's so angry. So depressed. So lost.

The only reason he's not floating face down right now is because of the frail men around him. He cursed them with this pain, and yet they saved him. That's not level five anymore. He doesn't really remember what level that should be. Was there an "I'll save your life even if you wreak havoc on mine" level?

His mind is leaking away.

How many times has she done this? This...lesson.

And what a hard lesson it is. The question is, will John learn? The answer is yes. Absolutely, yes.

The water stings. In this moment, he's as close as he's ever been to letting go, slipping under the surface and saying good-bye. In his peripheral vision, he sneaks glances at his co-captives, watching them in their misery. He clutches both men closer, their faces falling onto his chest like lovers as they tremble, chatter, and suffer. Anchored between them both, John tries to share what little heat he has with them. With *A* in particular. In the harsh, hammering spray, John had been too stunned for his self-preservation to kick in, but *A* knew exactly what to do. He's saved him twice at this point. Three times if you count his quivering, spindle-ribbed body pinning John upright now. *H* is doing it too. *H* may be gruff—mean—but he's soft underneath, John's sure of it. A smooth talker too. Subservient and charming when he needs to be. He knows exactly how to keep The Bitch merciful, feeding them, watering them, and coming back time and again to get a dose of the attention she so desperately craves. *H* makes her believe he loves her, an act that may be the only thing keeping them all alive. These traumatized men have learned from vicious experiences, deadly trial and error, and John is done dismissing their hard-earned wisdom.

This is all his fault. They told him the rules, and he broke them. He knew what he was doing. Somewhere, deep down under his hate, he knew. He was trying to take control of his own pain. Trying to steer his fall from grace. Trying to fucking *Accept* and *Act*. But his actions were the wrong ones.

It's humbling. It's more than humbling. It's soul crushing.

This is all my fault.

No, wait, that isn't right. It's her *fault.*

...Isn't it?

He's not sure.

What happened to the other screaming stranger? John thinks, almost deliriously. *Will that be me someday? What happens in the faraway place that's not down here?*

It's frightening. Like a ghost story, but real. John doesn't want to be a ghost.

"I w-won't break the rules any-anymore," he promises, unable to keep his voice steady in the deep burn of the cold. "If we sur-survive this, I p-promise to be good."

A doesn't talk. He just burns with fever. He's been coughing right on them both. At this point, they're all going to get it, a boomerang right in John's face. He'd pretend his immune system can handle it, but he doesn't have the strength to lie to himself just now.

Their bodies are prunes, but not the good kind. Not the sickly sweet and soft kind. Not the shriveled, gritty kind either. Their skin is peeling off at this point. Every falter against the stone floor and you can feel it let go. Roll off. Split. The only solace is that the water is draining. Slowly, but better than nothing. That tiny bit of tarp John had managed to pull away from the grate truly mattered, the only real contribution he's made in his time here. Everything else has just been a pipe dream. A fantasy.

"I'll be good," he says on repeat, and feels *H*'s nails sink into the flesh above his carved letter. The man's fury knows no bounds, even while cradled here in John's arms, and John can do nothing about it. He can't do anything in general. Not cry. Not sleep. But he starts to imagine he could die.

He never understood that—how people could just accept death. Just look at your family and friends and say, "You know what? It's time." Now he gets it. Death seems like a warm hammock-covered beach in comparison to this soaking suffering. A mercy. Rescue.

John wants to be rescued.

Trapped more than fifteen feet underground, encircled by rocks and dirt, John rests his head against *A*'s and prays for God to let them all die.

THE PAST - INTERLUDE THREE

John never thought he'd sing songs. He neither sings in the shower nor along with the radio. He was never in choir and flunked elementary school chorus, which is indeed possible. Hell, John would barely sing "Happy Birthday" unless he reeeally liked the person (or if his mother threatened to withhold cake), but life is a tricky thing, making you do all sorts of stuff you never thought you'd do.

Beth is passed out in the comfy rocking chair, feet up, with a mostly swaddled Alex in her lap. The chubba-chub cherub had been suckling happily before both gave up and let sleep take them. John would like to do that too—it *is* three am, after all—but Amber's always been a slow eater. And burper. Given her little grunts and wiggles in her Daddy's Girl onesie, John knows for a fact he's got to get the gas out of her belly or she's going to wail the house down.

Amber's tiny chest is laid over the flat of John's palm, so light he could toss her like a pizza. Sometimes he does. She likes it. God forbid Beth ever saw it though. Seppuku would be John's only option.

He tap-taps on Amber's back to no avail, and her

squirming goes to defcon three. We're in danger territory. His tap-taps become thump-thumps, which still freaks him out a little. He can throw her to the clouds, but he's terrified to break her otherwise. So, to soothe himself as much as her, he starts humming, then singing. It's the song his mother used to sing to him when he was little. The one that Nonna used to sing to her. The one that traveled straight off the boat from Italy and got bastardized with English somehow. It reminds John of snuggles and cuddles and overall goodness.

"Dorme, dorme, dorme. Goodnight and sleep well, my love. Dorme, dorme, dorme. Angels are watching above. 'Til the dawn on tiptoe steals over your windowsill, may every bright star attend thee and befriend thee with its light. With every note that I send thee, dorme, dorme my love. Goodnight."

Ah! He's tearing up! Why do these kids always make him feel like he's going to explode with love? It's only a matter of time until he cries over Hallmark commercials! This is pathetic. He's so glad his wife is out cold. She'd tease him until the day he dies.

Still, he keeps singing, his crappy voice cracking through his weepy-dad vibes. It's working though. Amber is relaxing into it. She's making softer cooing sounds, but that's about it...until the most vicious belch he's ever heard tears from her throat along with a good amount of spit up.

John gapes at her and she blinks back, no issues on her side. He's basically glowing with pride over his super-awesome-nighttime-win right now, Dad Number One branded on his chest. Maybe he'll take to singing more often.

Wiping her milky face with a cloth, he smirks at her. "I told you I was gonna make you burp, didn't I?" He curls her into his arms and nuzzles, enjoying her baby-head smell. "Didn't you know? Resistance is futile."

Popsicles are drippy things, but at least they're mostly water. Creamsicles, on the other hand, are mostly milk. Or sherbet. Or something else sticky and miserable. Which is why it sucks that it's running down the twins' chins, all over their hands, and into their damn laps. Beth grimaces as Amber flails, trying to catch onto a curl of her hair. Her giggle and subsequent, "Mama!" is met with a sigh that's one part his wife's annoyance deflating from the overwhelming cuteness, and a second part a quiet plea for help.

Hands already full of baby wipes, John's trying to clean Alex's face while she simultaneously tries to re-slather it in another layer of wannabe ice cream. He looks at his wife with a lift to his eyebrows and a shrug, basically a silent "Whaddya want *me* to do?" One at a time. That's how it works with twins.

Their little ladies are late bloomers. The interwebs say that their last molars are supposed to have come in by the age of four, but tell that to the two teething monsters gnashing at their treats, numbing the backs of their gums with freezing cold even though it's already winter outside.

John shivers. It's not that he hates the cold; not really. His mother always told him, "There is no such thing as bad weather, only bad clothes," and he believes it—as is represented by his choice to wear the questionable home-knit scarf his wife made him—but he also believes that the temperature at three p.m. is different from the one at seven p.m.. Forty degrees can dip to twenty pretty damn fast in his book. It's miserable out right now. He really needs to move south. Somewhere that dips no lower than sixty. Fifty-five, tops. That's still shorts-wearing weather.

"All done." He flicks Alex's wooden creamsicle stick to the

ground and hefts her out of her carriage. Any trip longer than thirty minutes and they need a damn stroller to avoid the children grabbing their ankles and moaning like they're being tortured, leaving their parents to drag them across the grass.

Beth is still working on Amber when he latches his little goober into her car seat, trying desperately to avoid her irreparable hands as she paws at him for the seatbelt.

"Lemme!" Alex insists.

"I could, but then we'll be here for an hour."

She huffs.

John raspberries her forehead and mutters, "Daddy's cold, precious. I want to go home. Wanna put the fires on with me?"

And he's met with a gasp of joy and a grin.

"Fires?" Amber says, hopping in on the other side. "Yes, yes, yes!"

"Really, John?" Beth groans, but it's with amusement written all over her face.

"What? They've been so good today!" His voice drops to something low and nasal as he babies them. "Hwaven't you been gwood today?"

There are so many "yups," it's borderline terrible.

"See?" He grins at his wife. "The children have spoken!"

"Fine." Beth snorts at him, doing Amber's latches. She points a finger playfully. "But I'm not picking it all up!"

"Wouldn't dream of it, darling," he teases, knowing full well she will be. After all, it's her mess to begin with. Beth is a collector of scented candles. Pine burns at Christmas, apple pie at Thanksgiving, pumpkin on Halloween. There are a variety of "beach" smells for the summer, though he doesn't think they smell like a beach at all, and assorted flower scents for the spring. The end result is at least fifty glass canisters of colored wax laying around the house.

Retired for three-quarters of the year, the candles have

gotta be lonely, right? In need of some attention. So John and the kids play mad scientist. John had loved to do it when he was younger. This most recent incarnation of the activity means that they gather up the candles, all million of them, and start to light them in batches, pairing scents together to try and find an inoffensive combination. Oddly enough, too many flower scents together make John want to die, but an apple/pumpkin mix makes him want to *bake.* He is not a baker by any means—he can barely dunk a cookie in milk without it melting apart—no, instead he buys pies at the grocery store and sticks them in the oven for 5-7 minutes to warm them up. Who needs a stupid, smelly candle then? No one! Not when they have the real thing.

If he leaves the pies in for even a tad too long though, they come out black at the edges, and then the kids won't touch them. He learned that the hard way. Once he and Beth were drowning in a pile of pies for a hot minute with no ravenous twaddlers to help devour them.

"I see that look on your face, husband." Beth's pet name/insult for him. "I'm getting stuck with cleaning it again, aren't I?" She gets into the passenger's seat, looking at him askance and knowing him all too well.

"No! Not entirely!" John reaches over and pecks her on the temple. "I'll clean up one all by myself."

She thwacks his chest halfheartedly and kisses his red, chilled nose. "Take me home, you jerk." Which may or may not be an invitation for some action later, given the look in her eyes.

The twins are a handful, but maybe someday soon they'll make a third. John wants a big family. He's still got space in his heart for lots more.

———

"Jump, sweetheart, come on!" John holds his arms out in invitation, spreading just as wide as his smile.

Alex looks at him warily, her jet-black hair woven into one of those fishtail braids, too complex for any mere mortal man to do. Her big blue eyes stare at him in tense anticipation while Amber puts her hands over her mouth, stifling a nervous giggle when Beth beckons them both.

"You can do it, sweethearts! I know you can!" she says, trying to encourage them to play along. Poor Beth is only stared at, but it doesn't take away an ounce of her enthusiasm. The twins, however, are skeptical at best.

"I'm not ready, Daddy." Alexandra looks down, her eyes frozen to the shimmering surface with concern.

Dustin had left on vacation and given them carte blanche over the use of his pool while he was away. That guy is a good neighbor, though his wife can go bite the big one.

The back yard is nicely manicured, and the kidney-shaped pool is a crystal-clear blue. The textured turquoise paint on the bottom makes the water look like something straight out of a Caribbean vacation TV commercial. John's going to take his girls on one of those trips someday, all three of them. Beth makes good money, and they've been smart about saving it lately. If there's anything you should splurge on, it's happiness. Experiences. Life. Love.

"If your mom can swim, honey, then so can you." He looks at Beth and winks, making her roll her eyes and snicker, working her arms back and forth and floating a bit before dipping her head under the water. When she comes up, her curly hair is almost completely straightened, and the sun kisses her smattering of freckles with its warmth. If they stay out here for too long on a summer day like this, an entire new constellation of speckles is certain to bloom over her nose, cheeks, and shoulders. John has already decided to smooch every last one of them.

"See, sweethearts?" Beth cajoles the twins. "Even if you go under, it's okay!"

"And we've got you." John is supposed to be looking at the girls, but he's looking at his wife. Sometimes he catches himself doing it for no reason. She doesn't mind. It usually makes her bite her bottom lip and blush. Too bad she's not catching him in his transgressions right now. He likes making her cheeks turn pink.

Finally turning to the twins, he says, "You don't need your swimmies. You're big girls now."

They all look back to the outdoor lounge chairs, the kind with the plastic slats that leave funny lines on your skin when you finally get up. Lying there, silent in the shadows, are their little inflatable arm tubes, pinker than possible. Hello Kitty runs rampant over them, the little bowtie on its head mocking the girls' attempt at bravery.

"Hello Kitty wants to come," Amber whines.

What she really means is, "*I* want Hello Kitty to come. Preferably cinched up to my armpits."

John says, "You're five now! *Five!* Do you know how old that is in dog years?"

He might get them a dog. If he does, he wants it to be a big one. Loyal. A German Shepherd or a golden retriever maybe.

"What are dog years?" Amber asks, suspicious, and rightfully so.

Alex purses her lips, ignoring her sister. "How old is it?"

Well, damnit, he didn't think she'd actually ask. Is it seven years per human year? Or does it kind of stagger? Like one year is equal to one year, but five years is equal to forty?

John does the adult thing and lies through his teeth. "A hundred!"

Both girl's eyes go wide and *Whoa* in unison. To them, a hundred may as well be infinity. An almost painful joy winds its way around John's heart, making smiling as natural as breathing. The sky beams down from overhead and he beams up from the water.

"And do you know what hundred-year-old dogs do?" Beth chimes, mischief in her voice. She's met with two children blinking at her. "They get brave and theyyyyyyy...*JUMP IN!*"

With a big wave of her arms, she splashes at the girls, making them squeal out cries of shock and laughter.

Swim-walking to the edge, John reaches far out and cups Alex's ankles. "You know I'll never let anything happen to you, right?"

She nods, shy and bashful. Beth comes up beside him and wiggles Amber's toes with a grin, making her dance away while making funny noises. Still, John keeps his eyes locked on his firstborn (by all of three minutes). "I believe in you, kiddo. I know you can do anything."

Alex's eyes get firm and John knows he's got her. He backs up a few steps in the water to give her space before lifting his eyebrows in challenge. His little one casts a last longing glance at her omnipresent nightmare Hello Kitty swimmies before looking at him with something akin to a glare. Next, she nods at Amber, and her twin gets with the program, both of them readying their little bodies.

Beth's arms go up first. "Come on, Amb, I've got you."

John's are out a split second later to catch the other twin. "One. Two..."

"THREE!" Beth yells, and the girls go for it.

They barely go a foot away from the edge as they launch themselves into their parents' awaiting embraces. It's one of those moments that goes in slow motion, housing an eternity in a split second. John can see them all so clearly.

The girls are wet from a solid hour of swimming already, puttering around in the shallow end and making good use of the squirt guns. Each fleck of water that flings from their bathing suits beads in the air, sparkling as it hovers, waiting for time to flow normally again.

John's gaze latches onto every cascade of their hair, tresses like galaxies, deep dark with tiny flecks of dandruff he scrubs menthol shampoo into. He is going to get rid of that flakiness before first grade starts, so help him. It's not called *shampoo* though. The girls call the blue-green gobs he smears on their heads *tinglepoo,* which may or may not be the most hilarious thing he's ever heard.

He's in love with the way Alexandra cinches her eyes, all ten fingers clamping her nose shut. He's equally in love with the way that Amber does neither of these things, open-eyed and grinning like a loon, ready to inhale some chlorine. His brains and his brawn in two sweet little packages.

He should close his eyes so that he doesn't get pool water in them, but John won't miss a millisecond of this forever moment. His cheeks are dimpled as he waits endlessly for them to hit the water. To crash into him without mercy. This is one of the most perfect moments in his entire life.

When they touch down, that eternal moment ends, leaving both parents and children laughing and spinning in the water. John and Beth each hold one baby tight, praising them to high heaven. So many "Good girl"s and "I love you so much"es and "I'm so proud of you"s.

John hoists Alex from the water's skin, setting her on the edge again and letting her get her bearings. She'd dunked under for a split second, and John is ready for her to have a rough moment. Behind him, Beth and Amber's sounds collide together, dancing, reverberating, echoing, but John's focus is on his stunned little girl.

She looks at him. Really looks at him. He's ready for her to start bawling, but instead, her pink lips open in awe.

"Can we do it again?"

John's eyes crinkle. "As many times as you'd like."

Love

John jerks from his zombie-like daze, launching himself slightly from the wall and jostling the two men in his arms. It opens *A*'s sores again, the ones that live in the hollows of his armpits, rancid, festering wounds that will never heal.

"The dirt..." John mumbles as if in a dream. Perhaps he's in one.

The water is at hip-level now and the sun beats down on it, making the ripples glisten with a light so bright it hurts his eyes. *H* blinks at him, obviously atrophied from standing for hours on end. *A* remains asleep, an inferno propped up in John's haphazard embrace.

"What about it?" the other man says, one last shudder roaming through his chilled body before he hoists himself up, stiff and weak, and immediately almost goes down in the water, catching himself only at the last second.

Clutching *A*, John turns to look at the set of blocks he's relieved of their mortar. "I've been holding back on digging because we didn't know what to do with the dirt. How to hide it from her." He looks at *H* with wide eyes. "All I have to do is put it in the water. Dilute it. Flush it away. Keep me shiny and clean."

This would be the most crucial benefit of the oversized plunge pool they've found themselves in, one of a growing list of silver linings. The first was that John and the others have been drinking so extensively that their stomachs are distended and queasy from the intake. That doesn't stop them though. The second benefit was that peeing next to one another creates a miraculous moment of warmth, ebbing out with a shadow of reprieve before the cold sets back in. They tried to time it so they didn't waste the precious heat all at once. It made the water around them taste funny though.

"Did you know the ocean is salty because of whale sperm?" John lets out the non sequitur in awe, letting it hang in the air as he stares toward their no-longer-hiatused escape route. Their hidden tunnel of salvation.

"Crazy." Still rocking on the balls of his feet, *H*'s eyes are closed as his lined face turns toward the sun. "You're crazy."

"Aren't we all?"

There is the tiniest laugh. A shrill titter of a thing. "Maybe."

John can't take his eyes off the bricks, absently lifting water in the cup of his hand and bringing it to his mouth for a gulp. He does the same for *A*, but the man doesn't take it, preferring to keep up his sleeping beauty routine. Changing tactics, John rests a cool hand on his forehead out of paternal habit more than active thought. "Do you think she'll come back today?"

"She might. She might not," *H* says. "Depends on her mood."

John didn't really expect him to know, but he glowers anyway. "If I'm going to do this, I need a timetable. I need to know when it's safe and get it done before the water drains. We're on a deadline now."

It's like *H* hears him for the first time, truly hears him instead of being half lost in his haze. "You think we can do it?" It's not just a question really. It's hope, doubt, terror, and anticipation all at once. John can hear every note in *H*'s voice for exactly what it is.

"First, I need to move the dirt. Which means I need you to hold him." He nods down to the unconscious man in his arms. "Now, before it gets too cold again and you can't handle it."

"Whale cum really makes the ocean salty?" *H* marvels, his eyes blinking at odd intervals.

Completely serious, John nods. "They spew out, like, gallons of it all at once. As long as they're alive, the ocean will always be salty."

"God save the whales," *H* deadpans. His teeth show when he grimaces. "I'm never going swimming again."

John looks down all around him and swallows his panic, seeing the depths as a murky monster eating him up one inch at a time. "Neither am I."

That's when two wrapped loaves of bread and a zip-lock bag of meat get tossed over the lip of the well and land in the water. *H* snatches them in fear, looking up and likely wondering what was heard. Escape plans or the wins and woes of the ocean?

"Baby?" he calls up, letting his voice ricochet off the stone walls. "Baby, are you okay?"

Yeah, John thinks. *Let's make this a quick chat if you don't mind. In and out. Get the daily viewing out of the way so I can get to work...as best I can, anyway.*

"I'm still mad at you!" comes over, distant and sad. Whiny almost.

"I know, baby, and you have every right to be!" *H* tries to placate her, hands over his heart in earnest.

"You didn't stop him! You didn't even try!" She sounds

close to tears. "I asked you to and you didn't listen! Whatever is happening to you down there is not my fault! It's yours!"

"I'm sorry. I'm so sorry!" *H* chokes out. Suddenly all the water in his system floods down his face in red, ruddy tears. He's quieter about it than she is, but it still happens. One of those irrational moments that takes hold of them all down here in the Fishbowl, the moniker now more literal than figurative. "Would you like to stay with us? Talk to us? Give me a chance to make you feel better?"

Her voice sounds softer. Quieter. As if shifting the blame has soothed her somehow. "Tomorrow. Maybe. If...if I remember."

Clutching the loaves of bread against his chest, *H* stage-whispers, "We miss you. *I* miss you."

Little fingers loop over the side of the well and round eyes peep down. *H* smiles, putting on the best show of his life.

"There's my girl."

John can never see her too well at this time of day.

"I miss you too," she says, sweet as sugar.

John clears his throat and looks up at *H,* not sure if he should open his big fat mouth again. He wants to throw up, but he also wants, very, *very* much, to be a good boy. At least until he is a very, very bad one.

H nods at him and John speaks. His voice crackles with the increase in volume, still raw from his screaming fit. "For... for what it's worth, I'm sorry too. I don't... I'm adjusting. But you coming back here even after what I did...? It means so much." In an instant, he's teary too. "I get it now. I knew the rules, but I was scared and angry. I lashed out at you, and it was unfair. I'm sorry. I'm not angry anymore. I—"

"But you're still scared?" she asks, jumping into his monologue.

He looks at *H* with wet, saucer-shaped eyes and the man just stares back.

Make or break time. What's the right choice? What's the hard-won lesson? What were the rules?

I have to earn trust. I have to own my mistakes and admit I failed. I need to take responsibility. I need to own it.

"Yes," he says, his voice hitching over the lump in his throat. "Yes, I'm scared. But that doesn't mean I'm not learning." He looks at her, as honest as he's ever been. "I'm not going to do that again. I'm going to be nice."

"But you're scared?" she repeats, as if wanting to be absolutely sure.

He sniffles but doesn't bother wiping his nose, undercarriage shrinking under her regard in the cold water. "Yes."

She lifts herself up onto her elbows, her torso fully visible as she looks down at them. "Good."

His eyes drop to the shimmering water. He still sees her indirectly, reflected from above with little eddies tearing through her face and warping her features. After a pause that has his heart in his throat, she finally speaks again.

"I'm done with you for the day. I have chores to do, and tomorrow I have work. It's going to be a long trip. I'll be gone a few days"—she looks down at *H*—"but I'll come and see you before I go."

John hoists up *A,* who'd been sliding down his slippery skin. The water sloshes around them a bit as the man sags against him. The Bitch startles and leans over as far as she can without toppling in herself, finally and truly looking at the state of one of her precious firsts after she'd ignored his ruinous plea for help.

"What's wrong with him, John? What happened?"

He winces under the sound of his name and answers as a knee-jerk reaction. "Fever. He-he has a fever."

"How hot is he?" she asks, borderline panicking.

John just shakes his head, sniffling again. "Hot. Really, really hot."

With purpose, he takes water in his hand and tries to press it against *A*'s mouth again, although to no avail. When it doesn't work, John rests his cool fingers against the man's forehead once more, sweeping his frizzled dreadlocks to the side, hushing and shushing. It's a little bit of a show for *A*'s sake, something to earn their captor's sympathy. John wants to help him, he truly does, but in a detached sort of way he also wonders... He'd asked God to let them die, so is his wish being granted for the first of their crew? If so, how will *H* go when his time comes?

"No!" she cries. "No, no, no!" Her hands go to her mouth, and she shakes her head. After a moment, her fingers shrink into angry fists, but her voice is nothing but fear spoken through clenched teeth. "I'm taking him up." She glares at *H*. "You know what to do."

"Of course," he answers, still holding the food, trying not to let it soak.

She turns on her heel and dashes away. John still can't count the footsteps.

"What's she doing?" He can't hide the dread from his voice.

H ticks his chin in *A*'s direction. "She's going to help him."

John laughs. It's only a huff, no more, but then he smiles. "Really?" He snuggles *A* closer, cradling him as best he can.

Smiling at him the tiniest bit, *H* nods. John leans his nose into *A*'s filthy hair and starts crying again, but happy tears this time. What was he thinking? This is better than dying. If *A*'s healed, maybe he can come with them when they get out of here. Maybe John can still make that dream come true—the one where they all have a picnic together in the sun and the grass. He'll never understand what it's like to be them, but he still knows better than anyone else ever will. That means they're brothers for life. Level ten all the way.

"Here's how it's gonna work," *H* says. "She's gonna come with the truck. It has a winch. You might feel some sort of way when you hear the sound of it. It might remind you of your arrival, yeah?"

John can't help but cringe, tucking a bit into the water.

"But we don't have time for that. If we take too long, she'll get mad."

"I don't want her to get mad," he says like a baby.

H ignores him. "She's going to drop down a hammock. At this point she's gonna have to put it in the water to get it low enough for us to be able to haul him in. There is a scary part I need you to know and be ready for. You *cannot* fuck this up."

John nods rapidly.

"She's going to give us a syringe. It's filled with stuff that's gonna put him out."

"He's already out."

"Not enough. And he could be faking. *We* could be faking. Get me?"

John nods again.

"I'll stab him. He's had it coming for a bit anyway. It'll feel good to get the chance," *H* says, voice growling a bit. "But that's not the scary part."

"It's not?"

"No. When she puts the hammock in the water, you're gonna have to set him down. That means he's gonna go under the water for a second until she can get the winch up. You will be tempted to keep his head up or to not put him in the hammock when she says so. Do. Not. Do. That."

John's lower lip trembles. "But...?"

"*Trust,*" *H* says. "Trust goes both ways. She's gonna run for that winch and flick the trigger as fast as possible, but it's gonna take a split second for it to get him up and out. You *will* be obedient. You *will* drop him the minute she says so. At that point, you *will not* touch him again until she puts him back down here, and he'll be gone for several days. A week, maybe. It depends on how bad off he is."

"What's she going to do?"

Will he be like the screaming stranger?

"She'll keep him sedated." *H* reviews the man in John's arms with a cold and calculated glare. "IVs. Probably just meds, vitamins, and fluids. She'll wash him up. Probably cut his hair and shave him. When he comes back down here, he's going to look a hell of a lot better, but he's going to be a hell of a lot weaker for a day or two. Not moving for that long does something to your muscles, especially when we're like this." He gestures down at himself.

"H-have you gone up before?"

"Oh yeah. Not for a long time, but yeah."

"And…?"

H nods in *A*'s direction again. "Every time he goes up, he says, 'It was the best of times, it was the worst of times.' That sounds about right."

"Why?" John's morbid curiosity knows no bounds.

With a sick sort of smile, *H* says, "For some reason, it's the Viagra. As light as she is, she's still too heavy and too…enthusiastic when she rides. You feel like you're gonna break into pieces, but your body can't stop doing what she needs it to do. You're rock hard, regardless of where your head is at. It's the pills. You're chained up and half-drugged anyway, so you only get tiny snippets of it to remember her by. You still feel it though. It's a sort of painful, pleasure shame."

"She *rapes* you?"

H shakes his head. "I wouldn't call it that."

"What the hell else would you call it?"

H thinks for a long, hard minute. "Justice."

———

It's only minutes before John hears the truck, just enough time for them to have devoured what food she threw at them. *H* was absolutely right; John's panic is at level seven out of ten, but the other man just stares at him. Putting his hands palm-down in front of his chest, *H* lowers them to his belly and up again, letting his chest inflate and deflate in exaggerated breaths. John is quite familiar with the signal and tries to moderate his rapid panting. Even though he nearly caves into himself when he hears the metallic chain release from its spool with a bang, John tries to mimic *H*'s pattern of in and out.

John's nearly healed back flares in ghost pain and he salivates somehow, the pin-prick needle marks on his eyes and mouth itching as his nostrils flare. He locks onto the other man's gaze and refuses to look up toward the sky, not until he hears her sobs as she jumps out of whatever hell machine she'd dragged him here on, where he'd once sat with the squirming, squalling, very first screaming stranger.

The hammock is just that, white netting like the ones on the beach John had imagined. It comes down, dividing the light into little square patches and making John quake with fear as she feeds it over the edge, dangling it on heavy, rusted links. She's choking on her own tears as the slackening chain lowers into her death trap.

John can't help but wonder, *Can I climb it?*

No. That will only go very badly.

Learn your lesson, learn your lesson.

John has one chance, and this is not it.

Punctured through the plastic twine is a needle. It sticks there, out of place and surreal, like a messed-up, overdramatic painting done by some goth emo trying to make an unnecessary point about society. The barrel of the syringe is filled with something faintly milky. Sleep juice. Knock out juice. Likely the same as whatever she plunged into John's neck when she took him.

His nerves are fucking electric wires, keeping his muscle rigid like rocks. True to his word, *H* grabs the syringe unceremoniously and tips it needle-up, flicking his fingers against the plastic body with his eyes narrowed and his lips pursed. John's seen this on a million TV shows, so he expects the little squirt that happens as *H* pushes out whatever amount is needed to eliminate the air pockets. No need to give their poor friend a coronary on top of everything else.

"Bring him over here," is all *H* says, twirling a hand toward himself. Meanwhile, the hammock hits the surface and the white netting darkens immediately, losing itself under browning, brackish water.

I have to sink him in this, I have to sink him in this...

John keeps his breathing steady and decides not to think about it. Not this, not any of it. What matters is the woman above him, not getting her mad, not making her hurt them anymore. Right now, for all intents and purposes, the only things that exist in this world are his unwanted lover, John himself, and the emaciated *H*.

John doesn't watch, but he hears something like a pop and a harsh gasp. With all the self-control he has, John refuses to let his sensitive stomach twist. After a moment, he catches movement out of the corner of his eye, *H* holding up the needle and twiddling it as if to prove its emptiness before reinserting it into the hammock's twine.

"Wait," their captor instructs through her sniffles. John looks up as she wipes her eyes with the back of her hand, letting out one more sob before she counts down in her wobbling voice. From thirty to zero, John stands with a dead man floating in his arms. One who still breathes and burns but is dead anyway.

When zero hits, she tells John, "Put him in, will you?" like it's a favor. Like he's paying her a kindness. And maybe he is.

Trust and points. Earn trust and points.

John situates *A* as best he can, keeping his head as upright and close to the top of the hammock as John can make it, though it lolls heavily on his co-captive's neck.

Don't look at him, don't watch. Trust and points. Trust and points.

"Drop him, okay?" she asks, high pitched.

And John lets him go. *H* watches as he sinks under the water and, despite his self-inflicted advice, John mirrors him, coldly observing the man grow dim under the surface of their personal lake. But then there come bubbles...*blip, blop, burble*...and it makes John want to scream. To tear his own skin off.

I'm killing him. I'm putting his life over mine, and I'm killing him.

The winch starts, but *A* is inches under the water at this point. *H* stares down, his mouth a thin line with his jaw clenched so hard the tendons in his temples pulse.

When *A* breaches the surface, his mouth is gaping, and John can see the little pool of water drowning him there. It makes a gurgling sputter that John quickly blocks out. Out and out and *out.*

She's at the top, waving her hands in beckoning motion to the rising man, twiddling her fingers and trying to get a hold of him as fast as possible. The crank of the winch sends waves of gooseflesh up John's arms, but he stays straight as an arrow as she tugs *A* over the edge. There is a wet, familiar *thump-thump* of *A* crossing the truck's threshold, and it's the sound of nightmares.

John hears weird huffing then. Counting. Grunts, mutters of, "C'mon, you can do it," and puffs. It happens over and over and over…until there is a hoarse and wet round of coughing and retching.

"Good boy. I've got you. Sleep. Sleep and I've got you," she promises in fervent, hushed words from up above, completely unseen. "It's going to be okay now. Shhhh, shhhh."

There are no other sounds from *A.* John doesn't feel it though. Not the worry, not the fear. Nope. Nope, nope, nope. He *nothings* this moment. He doesn't acknowledge this moment. Across from him, *H* is doing the exact same…before he starts coughing too.

The Bitch outright wails from above when she hears it, but this time it gives John not an ounce of satisfaction. He brought this shit into the well, after all. Yet another thing that's his fault.

Then the truck's cab door shuts and the engine revs, the diesel scent throwing off its tang all the way down to where John stands, listening hard to judge the distance of the truck's drive—how far that engine needs to rumble until it cuts off entirely.

It works. This time, it actually works. Not only that, it sounds completely doable.

With a fierce determination, John stares at his wall.

It's time to dig.

———

The dirt, the dirt, the motherfucking dirt. John glances side to side, out of breath and nearly out of his mind as he pulls the stuff into the water around them. It's only to their thighs now and the mucked-up texture of it makes John feel like he's swimming in something much, much more than just their own piss.

He jumps at the sound of nothing, pointing his ear at the viewing portal above like a dog cocking its head to hear better. It does John no good, because there's nothing in the deepening twilight except for his own rampant paranoia. Just another night of misery down here in the land of Nod.

He chuckles to himself.

His trembling hands, so close to exhaustion, are nearly porous, and he's barely able to perform the acrobatics needed to make this work. At this point, he needs to jump up into the hole, rest on the flat of his belly, and pull the earth out when he slides back, raking pebbles over his navel and catching a nice set of scratches for his trouble. He's given up on trekking it to the grate for now. He'll get as much as he can into the water and then focus on mixing it in like *H* is doing now, waving his feet around and trying to make a whirlpool or Christ knows what. Cake batter, maybe. Even better, pancake batter.

John laughs again; he can't really do much else.

Without a word, *H* moves to rest against the wall, panting. It isn't cold like the previous night, but there's still a chill, so neither of them wants to sit in the mess they're making, though eventually they might have to. It's been almost 36 hours since either of them have truly slept. Dozed, maybe, but the need to stay upright and avoid drowning was more pressing than having sweet dreams.

As John thinks it, he hears a slight snore come from *H*, though it becomes a snort right away as the man startles himself awake. There's no need to say he's tired out loud. It's understood. It's a given. Irrefutable. If John is tired, then *H* is about to collapse.

"You need me to stop? I can hold you up for a few minutes."

"No." *H* shakes his head in a sleepy way, his voice hoarse, sicker and sicker as time bleeds out. "No, you keep doing what you're doing for as long as you can do it for. I expect the water to be knee-level or lower by the time the sun rises. I'll...I'll mix a bit soon... I just need..." He trails off into a little doze once more before jerking awake again.

John doesn't have time for pity. He launches into the hole, up to his hips now, and decides to stay for a while, making large, sweeping motions with his arms like a turtle in the sand, pushing as much behind him as he can. His shoulders burn and his head is woozy, but it smells good in here, even though he's almost choking on it. It's amazing that dirt could somehow smell clean. Maybe he'll find a worm... Worms have protein.

He's too tired to laugh this time.

This might make a nice bed, he thinks. *If she were dead and I didn't have to worry about her visitation rights, I'd sleep right here.*

Puffy pillows and fluffy blankets are more than out of sight, out of mind.

"Worming, worming, worming," John sings to himself before *pfft*ing and spitting, having gotten a bit of loam in his mouth.

The bitch of it is that he's got to go up at an angle. These guys can crawl, but it's not like they can parkour themselves out of here. The issue with that is that the surface is already high up as it is, never mind the added length a slope brings. John has no idea how long he's going to have to do this for, but he's sure he can't sustain it for long.

"Do you think she'll notice if I get buff?" he says sarcastically, his sound so muffled he doubts *H* even heard.

The light dims as he buries his exit farther with each land-locked doggie paddle. Crunching his stomach, he wiggles, trying to take as much debris out of the tunnel as possible in one go when he slips out. The earth falls into the muck liquid without complaint, its particles drifting and swirling together with the rest of the filth, inseparable. Untraceable. Maybe.

John tightens like a meerkat popping its head out of a hidey hole, ticking his head to the side again. Eventually he looks down instead, deciding it's his turn to mix. Maybe kick some of the clumps to the hidden altar. He needs to make absolutely sure he doesn't block the drain, but he also needs to make sure he doesn't open the gap any wider. He needs his timetable, no matter how crinkled and loose his skin is. No matter how many of his new scrapes burn in the dirt-water.

The white moon reflects in John's eyes when he looks up again, filled with hope. *H,* even with his eyes closed, has the hint of a rare smile that just stays there. John thinks the man must feel the same swelling in his chest until he says, "She's gonna know. There's evidence now. You're covered in it. It's in your hair, all over your face. This is gonna be over before it even starts."

"Ever heard of encouragement?" John says with a frown, still looking upward in order to stretch his neck, letting the ache in his shoulders have its moment.

"We're gonna die. She's gonna fix him up, then come back, see us, and decide that having just one fish in the Fishbowl is enough."

"You're untouchable," John reminds.

"To *you,*" he counters. "Not to her. Never to her." *H* coughs a bit before grabbing his beard and straightening it. A nervous sort of tic.

John scratches his own out of mimicry. "If it looks suspicious, it's just because you're only slightly disgusting whereas I'm *completely* disgusting," John muses out loud. "Huh. I can fix that."

Before *H* has a chance to balk, John scoops up a good bit of undiluted mud and flings it at him, resulting in a great *splat* and a squawk that should go into the *Guinness Book of World*

Records for The Most Hilarious Thing to Ever Happen in a Torture Chamber.

John's laugh is more like a villain's chuckle as the other man looks at him, shocked beyond belief. It's only moments before John reaches down, his aching back be damned, and tosses another mud-pie *H*'s way, splooshing it against his left arm as the man spins to the side, leg raising in the most universal defensive maneuver in the world.

"You son of a—" he grunts this time, and John pegs him on the side of the head, *H* only barely spinning his face away in time.

Giddy. Ohhhh my God, this is hilarious. "Rub it in," John states, goading the other man playfully, maybe as gleeful as he's ever been.

"You're gonna get us killed."

"No, I'm going to make her less suspicious. You've lived here for three years. Dust, dank, patina, dead bodies, blood, all sorts of bodily fluids have graced each and every stone in this place. Why *wouldn't* kicking all that up make us filthy?"

John's only earning himself laser beam eyes stabbing him in the chest.

"Then wash it off," John invites with his muddy hands gesturing over the brown water. "By all means. You won't have clumps of dirt on you anymore—though they do look fabulous, I must say, spring fashion-worthy"—he giggles like a schoolgirl—"but you might have a nice gross tinge left on you. Brown like a tan."

H looks like, if he could, he'd go for the tiny knife again, but that thing's unsalvageable at this point.

"Look," John goes on, still grinning but trying to be reasonable, "why would I be like this, but not you?"

It finally clicks, the man's brain deciding that it still has neurons left after all. John doesn't blame him. They're all firing at half-power. Or less.

Sharp sounds fill the air as Cujo barks.

Shit.

John's spine goes ramrod straight. Eyes wide, he sloshes noisily to the wall of salvation and reaches under the water for his stones. He needs to put his face in to do it, which should be a *Please God, No* moment, but there are more pressing matters to point his anxiety at just now.

H dives down for a swim as well, either washing himself or agitating the dirt into submission for all John knows, but he's presently more worried about getting his mirage back in place.

Brick One.

Brick Two.

Brick Three.

Just when Brick Four is lifted for insertion, John realizes that his paranoid imaginings have upgraded to a real threat. The dog isn't going for a rabbit. The dog is coming to the 'Bowl.

Shit, shit, fuck!

His biceps are trembling now as he works to shove the last of the stones in. This one is always a bitch because the others are already pinned. It's like a puzzle made of grit, friction, and sandpaper, yet on and on comes Cujo. Closer. Closer. Deep barks and snuffs. Dog tags jangling as it trots.

Please, John begs. *Oh please, don't let her come. Pretty, pretty please.*

And Brick Four sinks into position.

Frantic, he shoves them all one last time, patting, pushing, and nudging, trying to ensure the gray stones are in perfect alignment with not a hair out of place. Praying it's enough, he ducks down into the water as quietly as he can, scouring his fingers through his scraggle and rubbing brown filth off his face with more brown filth, albeit this kind with a waterier consistency, letting clumps turn into smears. *H* only stares up, kneeling in the water and letting it come up to his shoulders.

Both men move out of the direct light of the moon and huddle together as if for warmth, though it's not really needed tonight.

She has no flashlight. Cujo jumps up and puts its paws on the ledge of the opening, its snout and nails pretty much the only thing that John ever sees. She hovers silently, clutching a blanket over her shoulders.

"Hey, baby girl," *H* says, keeping all concern from his voice. "How are you holding up?" He clears his throat but is holding back a cough, John can tell.

She shakes her head without saying anything and John stays dead silent, not wanting to draw her attention. She's not really looking down just now, and that very much matters to him.

"I still have to go away. I can't reschedule all my work." She snuffles and hikes up her blanket, clutching it more closely. "But I shortened the trip. Two days and only one night. I was going to check up on one of my—" John hears the words *next victims* so clearly she doesn't have to say them aloud "—but I can't. I need to be with him right now."

H keeps his focus on her and her alone. "Is that alright? With your work, I mean?"

She nods sullenly. Her smile is self-deprecating. "The benefits of being part-time."

"Well, I like part-time," *H* tells her, amusement and fucking love laced into his voice. "Because then I get to be around you more."

Her smile is less sad this time, but she still hikes her blanket higher. It's not even cold, really. Maybe she's just cold inside.

"He'll be okay," she says quietly, even though no one had dared to ask. "He's...he's rough...but I've got what I need to make it better. He'll be with me for a while though. I'll be keeping him sedated. He's on a drip. A nice cocktail. I had to pull some favors to get it, but it'll be alright.

"Since I'll be gone for so long, he's bound to wake up before I can change out the IV bag." She sighs at the moon. "If he screams, you have to tell me."

Why? What happens if he screams?

"Of course, love," *H* soothes. "I'll do anything for you. That's why I'm your favorite."

She giggles this time, looking away like she's shy. She neither confirms nor denies. After a moment, her face grows serious. She looks down but can't really see them through the shadows. "This is worse than it's ever been. He's not just sick. He's dehydrated. Anemic. Malnourished. Jaundiced. He has infected welts all over. His teeth are..." She frowns and looks distant. After a beat, she says, "I don't want to do it like this anymore."

John has no idea what that means.

"Catch." She tosses something down and it lands in the center of the bowl, floating to the surface. "It's sealed. Fresh. I got the berry kind."

Inertia is on their side so the item bobs toward their position without them having to expose themselves to get it. John lifts it up, but *H* snatches it away.

"Vitamins." He says it like it's a prayer. It's the kid's kind. Gummies with a significant number of boxes ticked off for how many good things it provides.

"Mm. You get to keep the whole bottle. Take no more than three a day or you'll get sick," she says, as if it matters if they get a tummy ache.

Last meal? John thinks, swallowing.

Her tone is resolute. "I'm going to change some things when I come back. There's going to be more food, more water...just...changes." She lets a beat pass, thinking to herself before saying, "Here," and tossing down one more bottle.

This one plunks and sinks, making her groan and facepalm. "You might have to dredge for that one. Sorry. It's medicine. Keep it cold. Under the water should work. Take it morning, noon, and night. There's only two days' worth in there, so no more, no less. I'll refill the doses when I come back."

And with that, she makes her way without goodbyes, taking her terrifying mutt with her. John doesn't bother listening for the number of her footsteps, he's already got what he needs. Instead, he inhales a rough breath and dives down, fumbling hand over hand and refusing to open his eyes in the mess they've made. Eventually, his fingers brush against something cylindrical and he latches on, bringing it up.

A bottle of pink stuff with a little dosage cup taped on. *Amoxicillin.*

Looking at *H*'s face, the man is transcendent. Stunned, he doesn't even hold out his hands with greed, he just looks at the bottle like it's his newborn baby. John detaches the little cup, snaps the childproof lid, and pours out a slug of it before walking over to his co-captive. *H*'s fingers tremble as he reaches up, and he takes the medicine like it's the sacrament.

"She said 'sorry,'" *H* marvels. "And even though I didn't stop you, she's not going to let me get sick. She's not going to just let me feel this She's not going to let it hurt me."

It should be disturbing. It should paint horrible pictures about what she's done to *H* before. Somehow, it doesn't. Instead, living in this moment, right here and right now, it only brings John joy. She's being merciful. She's being kind.

Suddenly, John has hope for more than one reason. It's twisted, so very twisted, but it's also true. Maybe she can make it all better.

He hates her. He *hates* her. But, in this moment, maybe he loves her a little bit too.

———

John's muscles are on fire, and he just can't anymore. His chest hurts from gasping, his long fingernails are caked with black underneath, and his stamina has long since kissed him goodbye. He watches *H* mill around, pink bottle in hand, squishing the mess between his toes in order to work his fading muscles.

They'd shoved a good number of muddy clumps down the altar but, without realizing it, they must have uncovered a bit more of the grate in the process. What was once ribs deep is now up to their ankles at best, and though John's waterlogged skin thanks him as it firms up again, his soul is crushed. There's no way to clean himself anymore. Not that clean exists right now, not for either of them. They are streaked with lines of brown so dark, it's like painted stripes of shit turning them into human zebras.

John sits, resting his back against the stone, his tunnel concealed above him. His butt is in the equivalent of a puddle in comparison to what it had been. The dirt is gritty against his rear and the tarp is a blue mess under a hazed puddle of tan, looking much worse for wear. John has half a mind to rip it off and just drain the damn tub the rest of the way, and he would, if not for the inability to move.

"Sun's up," *H* remarks in passing. It's something to say anyway. Sometimes they need to hear sound, even if it's just their own echoey voices.

"Mm," John agrees, letting it warm up the insides of his eyelids as he lets them close. "She said she'll come back before she goes?"

It's *H* who hums his agreement this time.

"Why does she want to know if he screams?" *A* has every right to scream his head off, as far as John is concerned. Either in fear or whooping with joy after seeing the outside. Either one is completely valid. Maybe *A* should do them both, one right after the other.

"Because she'll kill him," *H* says simply.

John flutters his eyes open. "Why?"

The other man shrugs. "If you cry for help, you want help. You want help at that volume, you want it from someone that's not her." He collapses with a sigh against the other side of the 'Bowl before leveling his eyes at John with meaning. "She doesn't like it too much when anyone tries to get away." He flicks his eyes to the secret wall.

Of course she doesn't, John thinks, but it's thought without malice. Without sarcasm either. It's just another fact in a mountainous, tiring pile of facts.

They pass the time in silence, both nodding off every now and then while the grate slowly gurgles and glugs down the rest of the water. The place is truly a mess and John doesn't feel like looking at it anymore. *H* snores softly and John's head starts to sag. He curls over his knees, resting his forehead on them and wrapping his arms around, feeling his limbs pull taut with a deep and worn-out ache. His too-long hair brushes against his skin as the pads of his feet dig into dappled stone. He's matted. And bearded. And... Sleep takes him. For a moment, anyway.

"What *happened?*" It comes out half-disgusted, half-flabbergasted.

John and *H* both look up, heads wobbly and eyes begging for sleep. Not even *H* has the wherewithal to stand up for his daily ass-kissing right now.

"Hey," *H* says, his lips quirking up at the sides, though no more. "Good morning."

Eyes wide, she surveys their situation with a rote callback of, "Good morning." Polite. "How did you do this?"

John didn't think of this moment. It must be one of those

brain fizzles he's been experiencing. He was able to explain the possible reasons for filth to *H,* but saying it to her might be upsetting. Insulting. John opens his mouth, looking around, and then lets it gape a minute.

"Pretty nasty, huh?" *H* lifts his arms, looking at them for a second before letting them drop down. "Guess there's a lot more stuff hanging around down here than I guessed." He half laughs before leaning back again. "Sorry, sugar. We probably don't suit you just now."

"Did the sewer back up?" she asks, trying to rationalize it.

Not with as far down as that sonofabitch goes.

"I dunno," *H* answers for both of them. "Maybe?" He looks at the tarp for a hard minute but says nothing else, letting her draw her own conclusions. It's the perfect tactic.

That's right. We're just two drowned rats. What would we know? The more we try to make it make sense, the more she might try to think around the holes in our story.

H is handling her perfectly. John thinks of *H*'s hard-learned lessons again. Getting caught in lying must have brought hell down around his ears before now. John feels a mix of emotions that contain a shameful tinge of gratefulness for his experience.

"I don't know how to fix this." She sounds breathless, eyes flicking back and forth over every angle.

"You don't have to," John ventures to say. "It was our fault." He shakes his head. "*My* fault. I made the hose come down. But it's alright, it's just mud. It'll dust off once it's dry."

"No, it absolutely is not okay!" It comes out shrill, but not angry. "John, how can I fix this?"

He doesn't know how to answer, so *H* does it for him. "Don't worry about us, sweetheart. I don't need you to take a minute of your time. You've got to get to work today. It'll probably look better by the time you get back. We'll be drained and dry."

"Don't you think it matters if you're fucking filthy?" She looks at *H* harshly and John flinches. He can't help it. It takes but a second before she puts her hands over her face. "Sorry, no, I'm sorry. Old habits."

Confusion reigns over both men.

"Here," she says, ducking down. When she shifts up again, she has the feeding basket. John adores that basket. Every weave of it is a sensual promise.

She ties the familiar rope around it and lowers it down. John can't stand just now—if he tries, he'll fall—so instead he works his way over kiddo-style, hands and knees on the ground, rump in the air. *H* makes a better show of it, though he's still unsteady on his feet.

Reminding them, she says, "Today and tomorrow, but I'll be back tomorrow night. I thought about it. Over and over. I know what I want to do to help you, but I don't know how to do it."

Let us go? John dares to hope but quashes it right away.

"I'm going to look online tonight. You can find out how to do damn near anything nowadays."

"Can you?" *H* asks, his arms up and ready to receive.

John *pffts*. "The internet isn't just for porn anymore. Though it is also for porn." Both she and *H* scowl at him and he lets himself be chastised. "Sorry. Old habits," he tries, matching her. It earns a smile of commiseration, which eases him a little.

When *H*'s hands get on the basket, he gapes, grabbing John's interest. The man looks back up at their warden with wide, glistening eyes. "Really?"

"Really." She basically glows, resting her elbows on the edge of the well with a soft chuckle. "And from now on, when I can."

John forces himself into a stand and peers into the basket.

"Fruit?" It comes out tight. Choked up.

"Under it is a plate of pancakes. I don't have bacon though, just the same old jerky. I've got tons of it I've got to get rid of, but it's protein so..." She shrugs. "Better than ants, I guess."

She must know they eat them. John almost makes a joke about worms but holds back as goddamned hard as possible.

"I'm... I..." *H* stammers, speechless, and it makes her giggle.

"I guess I took your words away. In a good way this time?"

John's co-captive just nods, lips trembling. John decides to copy *H*'s previous question. "Can we eat it now or do you want us to wait?"

"Now. I want to see your faces." She places a cheek in her palm as she looks down, twiddling her hair with her fingers. It's like she's a new girlfriend cooking breakfast for her lover(s) for the first time.

They both basically fall on their asses in tandem, though *H* cries out a little bit when it happens, landing on some part of himself too hard. He pays it no mind as he picks up a single berry and looks at it...before promptly beginning to cry. He shoves it in his mouth and bites down with a little moan, then puts his face in his hands while chewing as slowly as possible.

John has half a mind to grab fistfuls. He'd love to shove it all down his throat without even tasting it until it's gone, but looking at the man across from him, he realizes he could never. Level ten, after all. Instead, he separates it into two piles, berry by berry. "Do you have a favorite?"

H shakes his head.

She *tsks* from above. "Yes he does. He likes strawberries. You like blueberries. You'd have them in your yogurt during lunch after a morning session."

John doesn't even prickle over how she knows such a thing. Honestly, John likes both, but he happily gives *H* every strawberry on the plate and takes all the blueberries, somehow knowing that's what she wants. He divides the rest next. Honeydew, cantaloupe, pineapple, grapes. It's one of those fancy supermarket mixes John's bought a million times, but he has no complaints.

"Thank you," he says in awe. "This looks perfect." He lifts the evenly divided fruit plate out and sees the pancakes, catching a whiff of their sweetness, and now *he* wants to cry. "Absolutely perfect." He means every word.

Looking up one more time, he asks, "May I?"

She nods, quick little chin bobs, adorable under other circumstances. Maybe even adorable right now.

John doesn't wait any longer. Neither does *H.* For the first time in a long time, they are happy.

THE PAST - INTERLUDE TWO

"I GOT IT!" Beth squeals, slamming the door behind her all too loud, likely pissing off their neighbor across the hall. The walls are too thin in this damn apartment complex. John's about to scold her when the reality of what she said hits him.

"You got it?!"

She doesn't even reply, she just hikes her shoulders up to her ears, balls up her hands into little fists near her cheeks, jogs in place, and *"KYAAAA!"*'s so loud that now the neighbor will definitely be pissed. John gives no shits.

"AHHHHH!" he screams with her, diving in and lifting her in the air, twirling her like a tornado. "Baby! Oh, baby, *YES!"*

She clings to him as he pinwheels her around the apartment, her laughter more frequent than her eeps. Now it's their downstairs neighbor that will be pissed. Again, literally no shits.

"That means we can afford the house?" he has to ask, needing to make sure the plan remains. He puts her down and looks her in the eyes. They're that sweet cornflower blue and squinted with joy.

"Uh-huh!"

"The favorite one?" He gleams at her.

"Uhhh-huh!" She grins back, her teeth perfect white and her lips ruby red.

"The utmost, absolute, live-in-this-house-until-the-day-I-die one?"

"Uhhhhhh-huh!"

"JESUS CHRIST, BETH!" He picks her up again and she squeals, making his ears ring, and he loves it. He loves her. He loves raises. Between his and hers, they've got it! They've got everything!

And that means they have another promise to keep to each other too.

He puts her down and kisses her soundly. A peck that basically smooshes her face. "I'm taking you to dinner!" he declares. "I'm wining and dining you." He points at the door like it's something to be conquered. "I'm going to wear a button-up shirt, put on man-spray, and I'm going to treat you to a meal fit for a queen!"

She lifts an eyebrow sarcastically. "Chinese food?"

He pecks her harder before muttering against her mouth. "Steak."

She pulls back with feigned surprise. "Steak?"

His wife is a terratarian. She will never touch fish—land animals only—but steak, *real* steak, not supermarket steak, is a rare indulgence available on only anniversaries and birthdays. Until now, that is. They're over a hundred-thousandaires now. Maybe not liquid in the bank, but in salary anyway. Thanks to the power of annual raises, his sales job will bring in something like 70k when he hits quota, and she'll now be bringing in a whopping 120!

Wait. Shit. That means they're almost *two* hundred-thousandaires.

He keeps smothering her with his kisses. "Mm-hmm. Steak. Juicy, delicious, expensive steak. And for you, sweet thing? I'm talking ribeye."

She melts, leaning back in his arms and closing her eyes.

"I'm talking pepper sauce and garlic butter."

"John, I swear, I'm going to orgasm right here if you keep talking."

He leans over and kisses her neck. "I can make that happen too."

"Oh really?"

"I consider myself an expert."

"I'm the only woman you've ever slept with, shouldn't I be the judge?"

"As the only woman I've slept with, you should know how hard I worked to unlock that particular box."

"Double entendre." Lifting her chin, she looks at him with playful, half-lidded eyes.

"And now I'm the ultimate champion of your downstairs, my lady." His lips quirk into a smile, an idea fully formed in his head. "In the bedroom or right here on the floor?"

She wraps a slim leg around his hip in a clear invitation, and he slides his hands under the curve of her rear. She grinds against his thigh and he's halfway hard already. "Can you even make it to the bedroom?" she teases.

"No," he admits, hiking her up one more time and tipping his hips forward into her core. She squeaks again, but in a lower timbre and with a completely different meaning. She runs her fingers through his hair with eyes sealed shut. Putting her lips on his, soft and parted, she gives him just the slightest touch of tongue before trailing those kisses over his cheeks. He's going to have lipstick kiss marks, he knows. He loves those. He may even wear them to dinner. Just like he may or may not keep her undies in his pocket.

Instead of fumbling backward the six steps it takes to get into their bedroom and then the two more to get to their bed itself, he takes the single stride necessary to align with their comfy couch before plopping her down. She almost laughs but he dives in again too quickly, sealing their mouths together and breathing her in. She smells like blueberry shampoo and tastes like mint, her bubblegum habit a cute leftover from high school.

"I love you," he whispers against her as he slides down to that sensitive place under her ear, easing down to perch on his haunches between her legs. "I'm so proud of you, sweetheart."

When he starts to suckle her earlobe, he can hear her smile as she takes a heavy, breathy inhale. He hums against her to make sure she hears his desire. Beth loves noises, and she draws them out of him earnestly. Nothing to fake when she feels so fucking good. He rucks up her flowy skirt and pushes her thighs apart with one hand, cradling the back of her head with the other. Her arms twine around his neck as he pets between her legs.

"So proud," he repeats, deep and low, as he finds her special spot and puts pressure on it. He nuzzles closer and puts his teeth over the crook of her neck, nipping. One of those pretty legs hooks over him again, the other staying wide to give him full access. She gasps as he twirls his nimble fingers counterclockwise, making him want to do it faster. He can feel the slickness building up inside her black, silky panties. It makes him ache. He bites her a bit harder, and she moans in the best way. "Did you wear these for me?"

She nods with another perfect, "Uh-huh." Officially the best word in the world.

"Good girl," he praises, flicking his fingers up.

"John," she whispers, high pitched.

"Love you so much." He sinks his knees down to the floor so he can worship her breasts, suckling over her thin camisole and leaving wet circle marks. She bucks up into him and he's throbbing down below.

"I want you," she says, her fingers locked in his black hair.

Gazing up at her gorgeous dusting of freckles, he smiles at her, a lazy thing, willing to take all the time in the world. When he slips her panties to the side, he curls two fingers into her with no resistance, making her hips surge harder this time as he pumps them slowly, promising silently to give her more. When she cries out, his nerves light on fire.

"Put a baby in me, John," she says, and he damn near finishes right then. He's wanted this forever. This was their next promise.

"Say it again." Removing his fingers, he puts his head between her legs and laps over her underthings, feeling the silk on his tongue and tasting her through the fabric. His thumbs loop under the edges to tease her, pulling the material taut. "Come on, pretty girl. Say it."

"Please. Put yourself inside me and stay. Don't leave. Make us a family."

"One more time, sweetheart." He bites the white insides of her thigh, and she gasps.

With panting breaths, his wife demands, "Come inside me."

And with a deep grunt, he tears those pretty panties in two.

Work For It

It's sunset before she comes back. They heard the truck long before they saw her, like she had it running for a bit while she did something else. Loading it, maybe? Does that mean *A* is coming home?

"Hello, down there!" It's chipper and high-pitched enough for it to echo, even though she's not pointed in their direction. Like a personal trainer getting them ready to sweat their asses off, she calls out, "I hope you had a good amount of sleep today. Tonight, we're gonna *get to work! Woo!*"

It's enough to make John tense.

She's grunting above them, and something metallic drags. John still winces when he hears it, though this sounds different from the cranking chain that dragged him here. There's creaking, and things click like they're snapping together before she sighs out a rough, "Okay."

A groan and scuffing is heard before a dark, circular shadow falls on them, blocking out a good part of their view of the orange haze in the darkening sky. There is a *flick* then, and John is immediately blinded.

With a gasp, he shields himself with his raised arm,

squinting up as the Fishbowl floods with light, something illuminating all the nooks and crannies.

"There we go!" She huffs, still unseen, and John is left wondering what the hell is going on.

He peers at *H,* who is similarly crippled by the beam cast on them. The man is blocking his eyes with his fists and his back is bowed in a deep cringe, as if he's a vampire about to burst into red flames.

Is it the light, or is something bad coming? Is this like the hose? Did we do something wrong? John swallows and looks up as best he can, preparing for punishment and trembling like an egg about to crack.

"Incoming!" The Bitch says, light as air.

Instinctively, John throws himself against the wall, back facing her in an effort to protect all the juicy vital organs swimming in his stomach. At least if his spine snaps with an explosion impact, he runs a good risk of dying fast, or at least not feeling sensations anymore. Cut those nerve endings right in half.

What's her stance on paraplegics?

Instead of a *boom* of imminent destruction, he hears *H* say, "Thank you, honey," in a tone so reverent, it hurts.

Venturing a glance behind him, John sees his dirty, mud-caked co-captive standing like a toddler ready to be picked up by his mama, eyes blinking painfully. The big basket is lowering again. It twirls on its rope and casts moving, dappled shadows in the white circle that blares down on them.

Baskets equal food, and John salivates on command.

"Thank you," he copies his co-captive. Twice. One more vehemently than the last.

The wicker is warm to the touch when he helps *H* keep a hold of it. Seeing inside, John laughs, almost giddy. "You got us fried chicken?"

She gazes down. What must be a floodlight casts a glow on

her face from the right side, keeping her visible in the twilight. "A little KFC never hurt anyone. Well. Heart attacks aside."

More than chicken, there's mashed potatoes with gravy. Biscuits. John has no idea if this is going to sit well or if his stomach will revolt after it's spent so much time clenching on nothing, but even if he's nauseous forever, he'll accept it with grace. After all, without strength, he can't dig anymore.

But...the water...staying clean...

Even as dirty as he is, he can't let it get much worse or he risks everything. The impossibility of his escape route sinks in again and his mood dampens. He keeps his face down so she can't see.

"Eat up," she says. "Quick, quick like a bunny. We've got some stuff to do before I need to go to bed. I'm exhausted."

They don't need to be told twice. Their mouths are stuffed before they even hit the floor, descending on her gift like vultures. John half wonders if *A* is getting a better feast than this, before promptly deciding that the man is more likely eating from an IV right about now.

Poor bastard.

"Welcome home," John says around his meal, knowing, somehow, that he's supposed to.

"Did you have a good time at work?" *H* asks. It's barely intelligible, his words peppered with the smacking of lips.

"You're sweet." Her smile is audible and John tilts his head up. With pride, she flexes a muscle, looking like Rosie the goddamned Riveter. "And yes. Complete success! I never lose a patient!"

"Patient?" John asks.

She giggles. "Didn't I tell you?" Flitting her fingers around as if she's conducting, she lilts in sing-song, "I'm a pe-di-atric neu-ro-surgeon."

All of a sudden, John doesn't want food anymore.

Her tone softens. "No one's ever been lost on my watch.

Not even once." She looks thoughtful. "Part of me wishes you'd lived nearby so I could have taken care of them for you, John. Maybe things would be different."

He wants to run away from this conversation. He wants to curl into a little ball and cover his ears. He wants to hide in a hole forever and suffocate. *H* gives him the side eye but says nothing. Apparently, this moment is John's alone.

It comes out like a whisper when he says what he thinks he's supposed to. "But then I wouldn't be here with you." Is he supposed to be remorseful about the idea? Wistful? Sad? Hopeful? He doesn't know what tone of voice to use.

"No," she agrees. "Still, I wish I could have saved them. If they were my patients, I would have."

It comes out like he's begging. "I don't want to talk about this."

"You talk about it all the time at conferences," she parries.

"That's different. That's a story."

"Everyone's life is a story," she says. It sounds sympathetic and his eyes water. He doesn't want her to be nice about this. He doesn't want her to talk about this. He doesn't want her to know about this!

He keeps his tone soft and speaks past the lump in his throat. "The story I tell is part of a show. Song and dance. I've told it so many times I can't feel it anymore."

"Maybe you need to feel it," she says. "Maybe you need to follow your own advice and stop running away. Radical Acceptance, John. See your demons. See them and let them go."

John simultaneously wants to hit her and be held by her. Maybe both, one after the other. Instead, he shoves his portion of food in *H*'s direction and curls his back, hiding his face behind his knees.

"Don't be like that. You need to eat." Again, it comes out

gentle. Cajoling. John wonders how far he can test his boundaries before her tone shifts.

H pushes his food back over to him, no words in his mouth and his eyes not connecting anymore. Bitter, John laughs a little.

Obedient little shit.

He calls up to The Bitch, trying as hard as he can to stay kind. Trying to treat this horrible, terrible, heart-wrenching conversation like it's a privilege. And maybe it is. Or maybe it will earn him one? "If you want to talk about my secrets, I guess that means we're already on level—what was it—five now?"

"No." She shakes her head. "I'm your level ten. I've been your ten since I got you. But you will never be that for me, do you understand?"

He nods, looking up at her as best he can with the light streaming in his eyes. "Then what level am I?"

Her face is stern as she says, "One."

John remembers well what that one means. *I won't kill you unless provoked.* Level one was where he was at when he first landed in the 'Bowl. The beginner's level.

For some reason, it hurts his feelings.

"Eat," she says again. This time, it's cooler. A warning.

His stomach threatens to heave what little he'd already taken in, but John does what he was told. *H* focuses on his own food, chewing methodically and keeping his head down. John has no idea whether the man is acting out of kindness, giving John whatever privacy he can, or whether he's mulling over what was said and picking John's life story apart. Though, after The Bitch's little tête-à-tête, it's more than just obvious; it's glaring.

Having said her piece, she pushes off the side with a sigh and yanks the empty basket back up. Next to come down is the familiar water bucket, which John unties without saying anything and turns to empty in the trough behind him. Next, the food basket comes down again but with...towels. Fluffy and baby blue in color. They both look up at her in confusion, but she doesn't explain a thing. Under the dreamy, soft, wholesome cloth is a replenishment for *H*'s meds, and he takes his latest shot of it with a hum of gratitude. Next comes cleaner. Spray bottles that advertise "Kills 99% of bacteria" and probably smells like fake lemons.

That's the power of Pine Sol, honey, John remembers from the old commercials.

"You can't do too much tonight," she says. "The ventilation here is bad. It will make you sick. Headaches. Nosebleeds. That stuff is basically poison. Tomorrow, I'm going out to get a few big fans and I'll run some extension cords down there so we can really scrub up."

"We're cleaning?" John asks.

"No, we're throwing a block party." He can see her cock her eyebrow, half of her face visible from the floodlight beside her. Her sense of humor matches *H*'s, it seems. The guy snorts a laugh.

"There's too much junk floating all around you. I know you guys aren't feeling great, so we'll go slow, but we've gotta kill whatever bacteria made his sores all infected like that."

His.

A's.

Apparently, names don't mean anything to her either, unless it's John's. Maybe he's too new to have lost his name yet. It makes him think of *Fight Club*.

"So tonight and tomorrow, we'll get some cleaning done. We'll also start on the faucet."

H's mouth drops open, almost comically.

"Food and water," she says, firm and undeniable. "I promise you these things going forward. *Everything else* is at my discretion though, and only allowed if you're being good boys. Understood?"

Both John and *H* nod so fast their necks might snap.

"I need your help, or we'll never get it rigged up," she says. "I don't know how to do this."

"You're splitting your spigot and running a second garden hose down, right?" *H* asks.

John imagines that *H* was once quite the fix-it guy. It's in line with how John pictures him, based on what *H* had said about his job. The grumpy bastard seems to be someone who likes to work with his hands, even if it's just waving a little rock-knife around to threaten newbies. He must have been so strong, once upon a time.

"Yeah," she says, puffing her hair out of her eyes and running a hand through her mouse brown tresses. "But I need the end of it, that screwy metal part, not to touch the wall or the ground. I don't want whatever's creepy-crawling down there to get inside." John can see her grimace from here.

H reviews the curved expanse of the gray stones, taking a minute to think. "We can tap something into the mortar."

John's hackles rise. That doesn't stop *H* from spewing potentially dangerous information.

"There's a weak point somewhere, I'd bet," *H* muses. "We can chip out the cement and wedge something in."

What the fuck are you doing? John screams in his head. *What* the fuck *are you doing!?!*

"If we can get a forked prong," *H* gestures with his hand, splitting his pointer and middle fingers apart like a fucking peace sign, "then we can tap it through and hook the hose head into it. Face it upward. Make it like a water fountain."

She considers. "It might still get stuff in the top of it though. Rain. Dust. Dirt. Grime." She has the audacity to shudder on their behalf.

"We can cap it." The man shrugs. "Doesn't have to be

anything fancy. A soda bottle cap even. We can just trade it out with you now and then if you're trying to keep it clean."

The ease and normalcy of the conversation is overwhelming. John is floating in a myriad of mixed emotions that settle on *surreal*. He feels foggy and lost in the moment, watching the two banter about something that sounds close to…gardening. John would almost think no one had just casually brought up the forbidden subject of his dead children, or that no one was currently showcasing The Flaws in the Fishbowl's Design, putting their tenuous escape plan at risk. Instead, John feels like he's watching HGTV and The Bitch is ready to add an innocent bird bath to her front lawn, surely not something as odd and nefarious as running a drinking hose down into the deep, dark well where she keeps all the lecherous men she doesn't happen to kill outright.

"Yeah." She taps her finger on her chin. "That might work."

With a hoist, she lowers down one last set of supplies: more towels and overlarge, violently purple rubber gloves— the kind you snap on when you do the dishes—complete with little frail-looking daisies printed on them. John's been stripped naked, starved and weakened, cut up and stitched, made to piss and shit in a hole in the ground in front of strangers, yet this is somehow a deeper blow to his ego than anything else.

"If you're done eating…?" she gives the not-so-subtle hint.

With that, he and *H* shove whatever's left into them as fast as possible and load the licked-clean containers into the empty basket. With an unexpected gesture, *H* throws the back of his wrist over his mouth and burps a good one. His eyes fly to The Bitch, terrified at his crassness, worried for God-knows-what, and tension frizzes in the air so hard, John can feel it.

She stares down for a hot minute, regarding them with narrowed eyes…before bursting into a belly laugh that goes on for much longer than it should. She leans over, her mouth in a gaping grin as she goes off like a loon, snorting and slapping her knee once for good measure. *H* joins her, eyes watering from the hilarity of the weird moment as he locks his hands over his belly, his body shaking and tears coming from his eyes for the wrong reasons.

It's out of place. Too normal. Incongruous. Does not compute.

Even so, John can't help it. Despite his best efforts, he grins like a fool.

———

The sound is so abysmal, she has to shout over it.

"I'M SORRY I CAN'T COME DOWN AND HELP! I COULDN'T FIGURE OUT HOW TO DO IT AND STILL GET BACK UP AGAIN!"

They all know better. If she came down here, the males at her mercy probably wouldn't let her get back up again. Even though their bellies are full. And she's being nice.

The sound is a cacophonous hum that blows John's eardrums out. Four industrial-type fans are angled at the sky, pushing the noxious cleaning-supply-stained air up and out while two more shove "fresh" air back in again. John feels like his dick is outright fluttering in this whirlwind. He stands over the altar, ready to accept the next bucket of clean water. His muddy towel needs to be wrung out for the umpteenth time, infected with the muck and schmek and stains of all the years she's kept people down here and beyond.

Last night consisted of scrubbing away until they couldn't anymore. *H* fell down from the fumes and John was shaking from the exertion. Maybe she took pity, but John wasn't sure.

She only said she was tired. Either way, they were grateful. How is it so easy to be grateful?

Today, John's shoulders burn as he works, and *H* has given up for the moment. The man leans along the edge, panting on his hands and knees, dizzy and lightheaded from all the work his frail body is being asked to do. *H* can barely lift his arms at this point, and the smell doesn't help either. Lemon and pine do not mix well. John knows this from long-ago candle experiments. At least they're not using straight bleach.

John has come to appreciate what he calls his Plastic Daisy May Purple Death Gloves. *H* had tried to work without them, and his hands had swelled. Girly patterns be damned, John believes he's better safe than sorry. He needs his hands.

They started as high as they could reach under that harsh spotlight. John was terrified that she'd see his special, sneaky stones, and tried to avoid them until he couldn't anymore. He'd mimed washing them for fear that they would jiggle, and thanked whatever God hates him for at least making her set up directly above the entrance to their tunnel, casting his sin in shadow. She can't know what they're doing. If she's putting access to water down here *and* feeding them, escape isn't a matter of "if" anymore.

John marvels at how he's managed to get them to hip-level cleanliness around the entire tank mostly on his own. Staring at the crippled *H*, John knows he's gonna need a break soon too. He has no desire to be laying useless on the floor unless he's sleeping. Or dead.

John's arms drop for a moment and his head reels, the smell and the effort getting to him. Somehow, for some reason, she takes notice and cares. She's been caring a lot today.

"HUNGRY!?" she calls over the blowing monstrosities.

"YEAH!" he calls back, shivering a little in the so-called breeze. He's not so sure he's allowed to say that he wants things, but *H* isn't listening, and she'd asked him a direct ques-

tion. That's okay, right? If he pisses her off again, she might not kill them outright, but she might decide to rescind her generosity in favor of slow, torturous revenge. For better or for worse, John now understands that the dying process can be stretched out for quite some time if she puts her mind to it. The experience is something John would like to avoid.

There's also a chance that she'll do something nasty to *A* if John misbehaves. He'd never forgive himself if that happened. John might only be level one to her, but *A* and *H* said he was their level five. That matters. Even after all this time, John needs someone to need him. He *wants* to be a level five. Six. Seven. Eight. More than anything, he just wants someone to look at him and love him. If not his dead children, if not his estranged wife, if not an enraptured crowd, if not a simpering one-night stand, then his new, cursed, emaciated family will have to fill that gap in his greedy soul.

Old habits do die hard, indeed.

———

He rests against the wall nearby *H*, the night having taken over the sky above them. John's about to nod off into sleep, but he has to ask. He was too tired before, but after a day of food, his brain is working again. If he doesn't get the words out now, he'll burst from the inside.

"Why did you tell her about the weakness in the walls? The mortar. Won't she get paranoid? What if it makes her look closer at everything?"

H is groggy. Their hard work has given sleep complete permission to take over, especially since they're being lulled by the one fan left blowing the air up, up, and away. "She was asking me how to do it without really asking. She does that.

She knew I would know, and it would have been weirder if I didn't fix the problem. Be glad. Tomorrow we'll have a hose *and* something to dig with."

"Huh?" John asks, though *H* just looks at him.

"The prong." *H* makes that peace sign again. "The back spike is sharp. It's basically a pointed wedge to jam into whatever. If you hit any rocks or roots to chip through, it would be handy, don't you think? Fingernails only get you so far." *H* frowns. "And they rip off pretty easy."

Well, that's an unpleasant thought. Still, a slow, sleepy smile spreads on John's face. "You wily bastard."

H grunts. "I can't do this anymore. Somehow, her...*niceness* is more terrifying than her sadistic-ness. It makes me afraid of what's coming if she snaps. If the scales tip, they're gonna tip hard, and I can't do it anymore." He sniffles, wet and heavy, before clearing his throat. "I don't want to die here."

John whispers, "You won't, I promise. I won't let you, okay? I'm going to fix this. We'll get out, I know." He scoots over and rests his head on his co-captive's shoulder. Miracle of miracles, *H* leans back too, their hair mixing together. John reassures his friend, "It's going to be alright."

Resting on each other, knowing they're not alone, both sore men drift off into sleep, and for the first time in a long time, John doesn't have a single dream.

———

The trough is up and OUT, and John is more than happy to see that mossy, vile thing go. He didn't even care about the winch and its scraping chain this time, he was just eager to put that wooden thing out of its misery. He has half a mind to tell

The Bitch to dry it out and burn it in a bonfire of joy. Thankfully, he manages to keep his snarky mouth shut.

The hose runs all the way down into the 'Bowl at this point, but isn't hooked onto the wall yet. John and *H* are too busy working under her direction, cleaning up the mess she doesn't know they made. Broom-like scrub brushes are gripped in their hands as they go to town on the stone floor—well, John does anyway. *H* is leaning against his pole, weak again, but he got a smidge further today than yesterday. He's getting stronger with consistent food intake, and that can only be a good thing. If they're both strong, they can take care of *A* when he comes home.

Mucked up bubbles reign supreme under John's newly slippered feet. They're like prison shoes—or what he imagines prison shoes would be like, anyway. They protect him the same way his Daisy May Purple Death Gloves do, though they aren't a matching set. For some reason, he wishes they were. It would be avant-garde. A naked man, dirty, bushy both up top and down below, traipsing around with purple plastic adorning his extremities.

He snickers to himself.

Once they have everything scrubbed up, the hose's last unhooked duty is to spray all this shit over to the altar and down the grate. Then the swirling fans will do their last appointed task before retirement, drying out the Fishbowl. Once that's done and all the equipment is out of the way, the new rules go into effect. Rules that seem like blessings.

Wash yourself. Everywhere. Soap and shampoo provided. Truly a miracle.

Brush your teeth twice a day. Floss. Rinse. She'd presented them each with their new toothbrushes, waggling them in the air in a teasing taunt. John has a Spider-Man one, God knows why, and *H* has Darth Vader. The man had raised his eyebrows hilariously high, and she'd giggled. It was almost beautiful.

"And he gets one too." She looks at the house with a nice smile, probably thinking fondly of *A*. Leaning down into the opening of the well, she lowers her voice into a stage-whisper. "I got him Tweety Bird."

John huffs a laugh. Why she got them all kid's brushes is anyone's guess.

"He's doing well," she says. "Bedrest, medicine, and I've got some nice salves that have really been doing wonders under his arms. He's still on a drip though. Pumping those vitamins in the easy way." She throws a wink in their direction. "But he's grumpy. I had to pull a lot of his teeth, and I'm not good at it."

John's stomach sours. Clearing his throat, he asks, "Does he miss us?"

H tosses him a look, but John thinks she actually likes it when he asks her about stuff beyond just herself. The topics may be...limited, but chatting this way seems like he's interested in more than just kissing her ass. Like he wants to have an actual conversation. He treads lightly, soooooo very lightly, but his question makes her sigh with a little smile.

"Actually, he tells me he's glad. That he missed his alone time with me." She drums her fingers against the lip of the well like a smitten teenager while Cujo runs around doing the unknown with its dog tags jingling.

"Oh!" she calls out, making both men look up with an instinctual cringe that she happily chooses to ignore. "I forgot!"

They stare at her in tense anticipation.

"I got cots!"

H mouths the word silently before it actually registers in his mind. "Like beds?"

"Yup!" She damn near wiggles with excitement. "Three. They're folded up so I can fit them down here one at a time.

There's one for each of you, aaand!" She draws it out for maximum effect. "Blankets."

John moans and it sounds downright sexy. "Really?"

"Uh-huh! They match your toothbrushes!"

Of course they do.

"And your undies and pajamas too!"

Now both men stand up straight with grins. How the fuck she got adult-sized undies with Tweety Bird on them, John will never know.

Master has given Dobby a sock, he thinks, delirious. This will make them human. This will give them *dignity.* John clasps his hands over his mouth and *H*'s scrub brush handle drops to the floor in a clatter of shock.

"And one more thing," she adds, looking like she loves this moment more than anything. "Pillows."

"I'm going to die," John says with his eyes closed and a grin on his face. "You're going to kill me, I swear! Seriously?"

"Yup!" She plays with her pigtail braids in childish glee.

"I love you," *H* says, hoarse and unexpectedly heavy in this blessed moment. "I fucking love you, baby girl."

Her happy twiddles get shy. If John could see her better, he wouldn't be surprised if he found her blushing.

"I know you do," she says. There is a pause. "I love you too."

And the two share a moment.

When John had his "moment" with her, it was overshadowed by something terrible, yet now she and *H* are enjoying their own one-on-one interaction, and instead of depressing and miserable, their circumstances are almost sweet.

Jealousy works its way under John's skin, and he just lets himself feel it.

"If you're super good today," she says, "I'll even get you stuffies. Something to snuggle at night." She hardens slightly. "But I'll still take them away if you're bad. I'll take *everything* away." She sounds distant about it though. Unhappy instead of threatening. She looks at them with utmost sincerity. "So please be good, alright?"

Again, both men nod fast enough to fucking flap and fly away.

———

It reminds John of his children, this strange, odd, uncomfortably pleasant situation. *H* lays in his cot, staring up at nothing and clutching his blanket in his hands, wringing it while thinking about who knows what. Meanwhile, John hugs his stuffy. It's a stupid, beady-eyed bear that his daughter, Amber, would have liked. She liked all kinds of stuffed animals as a rule, unlike her sister. For some unknown reason, Alexandra only liked marmosets. He remembers scolding her, "Do you know how hard it is to find marmoset stuffed animals? Nearly impossible!" But in the end, it saved John a good amount of money when they went to the toy store. He'd only get nagged by one twin instead of being bombarded by both. At the zoo, though, John was screwed. Alex wanted All The Things to make up for the times when she wanted None of The Things.

The memory makes him smile to himself.

He cradles his teddy-bear-baby, waiting for the instinct to suck his thumb to kick in or something. The dignity he thought he'd get with his Spider-Man pajamas is flimsy at best. Instead, he feels like a man-child, but he's so comfortable he can't really bring himself to care. It's fascinating how much his heart feels like it's going to explode right now. All he has are simple things, but it's enough to make him want to burst.

For the first time in what feels like a long time, he has

unlimited access to clean water. He has a thin mattress, lifted a few inches off the ground on metal rungs. There's a medical pillow that doesn't care how much he drools on it and a blanket that's fuzzy and probably a bit too hot for this weather. He now owns two sets of rudimentary, gag-gift quality pjs, with boxers to match. He has toiletries that include toilet *paper,* a significant luxury after what may have been a month or more. He also has one friend nearby, one more coming back soon, and a crystal-clear goal lodged in his mind. It's enough to fill his heart to the brim.

It's more than just that though. Not that it isn't wonderful and magical and completely unexpected and all, but more importantly, this moment makes him remember his girls. Would they have grown out of Hello Kitty pajamas and into superhero ones?

He's about to fall into a sea of tears, but he sits in that feeling. For once, he doesn't try to bury it. He doesn't try to squirrel it away or convince himself it doesn't exist. Right here, right now, he chooses to remember that he still loves his little girls. He's always loved them. Even gone, they're still his.

"Dinner!" Her voice is like someone auditioning for the role of Best Wife Ever. Hell, after today, John might even give her the part.

He and *H* rise in sync and pad over to where the moon shines down. She's late tonight. She'd said she needed a nap after all the hard work, and John didn't blame her. They needed it too. And despite having already slept the evening away, John knows for a fact he and *H* will go right back to bed upon her departure. It's been too long since they've slept this well, and they have some catching up to do.

H scrubs his eyes and stifles a yawn as the floodlight flips back on, shining over their new beds in a harsh light. The man's hard work today even earned him a tiny end table to put his medicine on. It's only a flipped-over laundry basket, but no one's complaining. It's damn near decadent.

"Want to know what I made?" she says. "Guess! Just guess!"

John grins up at her, stroking his unfamiliar beard. "Mor-rrrrrrre...pancakes?"

"*Pffft*. I said *dinner,*" she scolds, though it's meant in good humor.

H sniffs the air like a dog but there's nothing to smell but the leftover fake lemon crap. "No idea, baby girl. You'll have to surprise us!"

She makes a good-natured grumbling noise and lowers down the basket. Once it gets closer, *that's* when the scent kicks in.

"Garlic," *H* says with a happy sigh.

"More than thaaat," she warbles down at them.

The lifegiving basket lowers to chest level and John picks up a little set of napkins to find... "Lasagna?" He almost chokes on his happiness.

"Yup! Complete with melty cheese and fresh tomatoes from the garden."

John's tummy makes a noise so loud, it's painful.

Without a word, *H* drags over his laundry-basket-table and they sit around it, grabbing plastic forks alongside the paper plates filled with heaping pieces of gooey goodness.

"Not only that." She digs into the pockets of her jeans and tosses down a few more things. It's all John can do to catch them in time.

Nips.

Fucking *nips*.

Tiny little bottles that house the miracle of a straight shot of burning liquor.

"You. Are. A. *Goddess,*" John tells her, not looking up

from the vodka-filled salvation in his hands. Her laughter is a good belly laugh again, and he knows he's earning points.

See, H, I can flirt too, he thinks, like a brat.

He goes to hand one to *H* and the man eyes the stuff warily, shaking his head no...and John's smile falters. Suddenly he wonders if this is a test. Is he not supposed to drink? Is this a rule he doesn't know?

The Bitch shakes her head, guessing at his mindset. "He doesn't like it. Those are for you."

When John looks up, she's waving two tiny bottles of her own, amber and dark.

"We're going to celebrate our hard work today."

John looks at *H*, feeling a little guilty. "Sure you don't want one?"

The man waves him off. "At this point, I think I'd pass out after one sip."

Fair point. Between *H*'s three years of forced abstinence and his current body weight, hard liquor would probably poison the bastard.

"Alright."

They settle in and John notices that she's set up to eat at the top of the well, sharing a meal with them for the first time. Almost like they're equals. She chews with her mouth open a little. It's...humanizing.

This still has that same jerky in it, but the tomatoes feel like they're filling out his flesh with flavor. The greasy cheese is going to rock his stomach off-kilter, but he doesn't let that stop him. The pasta is perfect. There's a word for it, but he's forgotten.

"What's it called when the noodles are exactly the right mix of soft and hard at the same time?" he asks, not to kiss ass, but because he can't remember.

She talks with her mouth full. "Al dente."

He hums and crams as much in his mouth as possible.

"Where does the meat come from? Why do you have so much?"

H gives him a look again before just shaking his head and continuing.

"I butcher on property," she says, swallowing loudly.

Of course you do. But it's thought without malice. Almost fondness. A kind of, "Well, that's completely in character."

"It's basically a farm up here. I used to want to manage one, but life took a different turn, you know?"

Yeah, I'll bet.

"I love what I do though. I like kids. I feel like I can really get on their level."

As indicated by our new cartoon character clothing and other accoutrement.

John almost asks, "Do you have any kids?" because that would be a normal follow-up question, but that sounds like a no-no topic if there ever was one. Instead, he takes a tug of his first nip, not sucking it down as he normally would, but sipping with a satisfied hum.

"Like it?" she asks.

"Oh yeah. I've missed this."

It's her turn to think, "Yeah, I'll bet," but she gets to say it out loud. Sassy thing. Oddly enough, he giggles.

"Hey," she says down to *H,* whose meal is long gone and whose eyes are basically sealing themselves in slow motion. "You sleepy?"

He snuffles and sits up straighter. "I can stay up. Sorry, babe. I'm still here."

"No, no," she softens. "Go to bed. We're just going to drink anyway."

"And sing karaoke." John winks at his co-captive, receiving a good eyeroll for his effort and a sputtering laugh from above. "What kind of singer are you, tough guy?" he asks *H.* "You go for Guns N' Roses, or are you more into Britney Spears?"

H looks like he's about to deck him but gives up with a sigh. Trundling back to his new bed, the man lands face down, and the snoring is near immediate. It's adorable.

"Hold up," John tells her, going over to situate *H* despite his grumbling and efforts to shove John off. Even so, John manages to pull up his friend's comfy blanket and tucks his plush stuffy in close by, just under the covers.

What the fuck is wrong with me?

Still, it makes him smile. This is like playing the worst kind of house ever.

He collects the empty plates and loads them up in the basket before grabbing his nips and going to sit on his bed with a satisfied groan. Taking another sip, he smirks with mischief. "Now *I* am a man who sings Bon Jovi."

"Now *I*," she retorts, "would only sing karaoke at gunpoint. And maybe not even then."

It makes John laugh. For lack of a better word, this is nice. The temperature is good, his belly is more than full, and the spotlight brightens up the 'Bowl, calling attention to their new homemaking efforts.

"What do you do for fun then?" *Other than the obvious,* John thinks, looking around him.

"I used to knit stuffed animals. I was horrible at it though. Everything I made looked like a pig. Except when I tried to make a pig. Then it looked like a dog or something."

"Speaking of," John takes a sip and points upward. "What kind of dog do you have?"

"Oh, him?"

Apparently not even the dog is allowed a name.

She looks off to the side and down toward wherever the hidden monster lies, grinning. "He's a mutt, but I think he's mostly whippet. Aren't you, baby? You're a whippet, yes? Yes, you are." She gets that...tone. The one everyone gets when they condescend to babies and pets. It comes as naturally as morning hard-ons.

"No way. Whippets are skinny little things. That dog sounds like a beast."

She giggles. "Yeah. He's got a deep growl, don't you, sweetums?"

"When we do karaoke, Cujo can sing the death metal songs."

As if scandalized, she squeaks, "Cujo?"

John grimaces, hiding behind his bottle for a second, already feeling the warmth numb up his muscles. Worried for his life a little, he shrugs, chastised. "I didn't know its real name."

"*His* name." After a silence and a hmm of consideration, she takes a swig. "So, if we're going to have a nice little chat, tell me, John. Why did you cheat on your wife?"

His mood sours. *Getting right down to it, aren't we?*

This is immediately dangerous. He looks at the sleeping *H* and begs him to wake up. Why are his moments with her always such horrible ones?

Honesty. Own it. Face it. That's what she wants from you.

He thinks about it for a second. "I needed to be needed. I always have. For a while, everything in life was perfect. My family filled that void for me. Nothing mattered more than them. But when the girls—"

"Amber and Alexandra," she chimes in, probably remembering from his fucking presentations.

He swallows. "Yeah. When they were...gone, Beth—that's my wife—everything about her shut off. She didn't want food. Sleep. Light. People. Me. The therapist said she just needed time, but I was..."

"Lonely?"

And resentful.

"Yeah. It was selfish. I knew it then, but I sort of forgot

along the way. At first, I wanted to stop. I just wanted my wife back. I'd come home and she'd sit on the couch with me. We'd watch movies and TV and stuff, though I'm not sure she was really watching. Still, it was the only time I could get her out of the bedroom. I watched TV all the time to get her to stay close by. I wanted her to notice me. Be with me. See me. She never wanted to talk though. Never wanted to cuddle, God forbid anything more. She'd just sit on the other side of the couch, as far away as possible, with her feet in my lap. For some reason, it made my heart ache when she'd do it. Like I was already preparing myself for the day she would stop."

John drinks the rest of his nip and opens the next one, his tongue loosey-goosey since his tolerance level is down the drain.

"You know, the first woman I picked up looked like her."

She nods a little. "I'm not surprised."

John's not sure what to say to that, so he lets the sentiment pass him by. "The further in I got, the less I cared about what anyone looked like. All that mattered was that they wanted me. That I could see myself reflected in their eyes when they didn't look away." He gazes up at her and dares to ask, "How many times was it you?"

She thinks, even though John would bet she already knows the answer off the top of her head. "Three times with two near-misses."

He scoffs at his idiocy. "And I didn't even realize. God, I'm a dick."

"Putting it mildly," she chides.

"Putting it mildly," he agrees. "Beth knew, you know. At the end, she told me she'd always known, and she'd just let it happen. Thought I'd get it out of my system. When I think about it, that means that she never touched me because I was touching other people, and I was touching other people because she never touched me. Ironically self-perpetuating."

This is the worst conversation ever. He snuffles and wipes his eyes. If he could do it all again, he'd change it. Not just because he doesn't want to be in this godforsaken well, but because he still loves his wife. Ex-wife. "She was good, you know? She deserved better than me."

And that's the last thing he has to say on the subject.

"My husband cheated on me too," she says quietly.

He figured, but his ears perk up anyway.

"I used to follow him around, waiting for him to notice me. Wanting him to catch me catching him. I wanted him to feel bad. Apologize. Beg for forgiveness and stuff."

"And did he?" Goddamn his morbid curiosity. He bites his tongue as soon as he says it.

She looks at her drink and chugs the thing. "Oh yes. Turns out, he's a good begger."

John frowns. He tries to salvage this before it goes too far south. "I'm sorry if I hurt your feelings back then. I'm sorry for a lot of things."

"Like calling me a trite and mundane cunt? Like telling me what I do is so unoriginal, it's *boring?*"

His heart stops.

Own it. Own it. Own it, you motherfucker.

"Yes." It's all he can say. "I'm sorry."

She looks at him, appraising, and he looks back at her on pins and needles. They have an extended moment of silence.

John tries to control his breathing. Tries not to panic. "What's your name?"

She looks at him and her expression softens. "Do you know that's the first time you've ever asked?"

He holds her gaze. "Maybe it's because this is the first time I've ever seen you and not just myself."

There is a heavy pause where all they do is look at each other.

"Jane." She turns away, eyebrows knit. "My name is Jane."

He lifts what's left of his second nip. "Cheers, Jane. It's nice to finally meet you."

Her eyes water and her smile trembles. When she stands, gathering her plates, she tells him: "Level five, John. You've made it to my level five. I'll trust you with my secrets now."

Without another word, she picks up and leaves, Cujo's dog tags jingling behind her.

And for some reason, for some *stupid, unfathomable* reason, John is proud.

———

When *A* comes back, he looks a hell of a lot better. His hair is trimmed to a short, puffy 'fro and his beard is shaved. He's clean and smells something like Irish Spring. If he wasn't so rail thin, John might think he was a different person. Even so, he has rings around his eyes, is exhausted and sour, and his mouth folds in on itself a bit weirdly. It must be because of the teeth she took.

She brought *A* down unconscious, and they had to slowly pendulum him over toward his new bed so they could finagle him out without dropping his dead weight. It was hard, but not impossible, and John found himself having to feign weakness again. *H* still didn't have to fake anything.

Awake now, *A* sits on his mattress, wrapped in his blanket and sporting childish pajamas just like they do. Jane's jokes were real, and the dark man is swathed in obnoxiously bright yellow Tweety Bird faces, but he isn't as pleased about his wardrobe as John and *H* are.

At first, *A* won't talk. Won't acknowledge them. As much as John tries to convince himself otherwise, this looks something like shell shock. Feeling bad for his friend, but also feeling the deep danger that the man's attitude brings, John does the only thing he can think of.

"Hey," he says, getting down on his haunches next to *A*'s bed where he cringes in fetal position, cradling his own stuffed cat. "You feel what you feel right now—I don't blame you, I won't stop you—but you know you've got to get it together when she comes back, right?"

A shudders, but nods. "I know."

"Do you want me to hold you for a while?" John asks.

The man's lips draw into a thin line as he shakes his head, mussing up his pristine hair. "I don't want you to touch me. Please don't touch me."

John's heart aches, thinking of *H*'s story. "Did *she* touch you?"

The man's eyes are haunted. "She wouldn't stop. Unless she was with you, she didn't stop."

Darkly, *H* chuckles. "That explains her good mood then. Thanks for taking one for the team."

John tosses him a mean look, but *H* is still curled up in bed. Unless she's here, the man never stands up. It's like the sudden comfort is something he wants to enjoy every moment of before she takes it away.

Leaning close, John whispers to *A,* "See this?" He waves his finger in a circle, indicating everything. "It's good, right? She's also bringing down food every day. Multiple times a day. And *that,"* he points to the hose, "is unlimited access to water."

"You been digging?" *A* asks, so quiet John can barely hear, and all for the better.

"Yeah. There's a laundry basket I've been shuttling dirt in. Getting it all down the grate. She doesn't know the hose is rigged so we can take it down easy and flush out the evidence. There's no sign of what we're doing. I clean myself off real good, put on my happy jammies, and smile at her like there's nothing wrong. Everything is working. You're not gonna be down here forever, okay? And she's nice to us right now. As long as we behave, we're safe. Help me make it stay that way." Looking *A* in the eyes, he insists, "She's *nice.*"

Somewhere in the back of his head, John knows he's separating *Jane* from *The Bitch.* Jane is a wounded soul who feeds him, forgives him, and chats with him at night, their conversations getting safer and safer over time. *The Bitch* is a constantly poised scythe, and she possesses Jane's body when things go sideways. If he thinks about it like that, he can't blame Jane for the horror of it all. In this way, it's not her fault. He can flirt and be charming and smile in good conscience.

He's wrong. And he knows he's wrong. But it's easier this way. John can easily run from The Bitch, but he doesn't want to break Jane's heart.

———

The familiar cry of "Dinner!" breaks John out of his zoned-out stupor. He's shifted his circadian rhythm to sleep away the "nothing time" during the day, but boredom is its own kind of torture, insidiously working its way through your cells and stealing your desire to do jack shit. No one wants to talk or do anything except him, and it's too early in the evening to risk digging.

A has gotten back with the program, shoving his pain down deep for the sake of survival. He looks up to the circle that frames the sky and says, "Aww, you didn't have to!"

"Yes I did!" She *tsk*s without malice, grunting as she hefts up her basket. Cujo is panting somewhere unseen around her ankles. "And I made your favorite!"

Whose favorite?

"Beef stew!"

Not mine, then...

But he'll still eat it. Absolutely.

It's not encased in the latest meal-medium of a Tupperware for each of them, no. She lowers down a heavy basket that's basically a goddamned *vat.* John sees this as another test meant to size up his strength and decides to prove a lack thereof, guiding it to the floor instead of holding it up. There are bowls, real ceramic bowls, with metal soup spoons. John feels more human by the day.

"This smells delicious!" *A* says, rubbing his hands together while licking his lips comically. This must be made for him then. Maybe it's an apology. John wants to think it's an apology.

H drags over the familiar laundry-basket-table and they all settle in just as she does above them, taking a heap into her mouth and "ooh, ahh"ing when it's too hot.

"Oh, I've got another surprise," she says with her mouth full.

"You and your surprises." John is the only one with the balls to tease her. "What are you shocking us with today?"

She hikes up a goddamned boom box.

"You're kidding!" John's mouth gapes.

She lifts a finger with her brows to the sky and narrowed eyes. "Not karaoke!"

"I wouldn't dream of it." He grins, putting a spoonful into his mouth and letting out a pleasant groan at the savory, slightly peppery flavor. It's both too much and not enough at the same time.

H seems tired of being left out of the conversation. "What do you want to listen to, babe?"

She hums in thought. "Any suggestions?"

Another test? John bristles.

"I'm out of touch," *A* admits with a wry smile. "I'm in for whatever you're in for."

She looks at John as if he might say something, but his mouth is blessedly full, so he just gestures in a way that invites her to be their emcee for the evening. A grin comes over her face as she pops up her hand with a mix tape. How very old school.

"Ohhhhh, baby girl, yes!" *H*'s face glows as he scoots closer to the altar and closer to her, resting his bony ass on the grate, an uncomfortable position if there ever was one.

She smirks at *H* playfully. "You know which one I mean?"

"Best song in the world," the man replies.

She points at John again. *"Not* karaoke." After a bit, she looks away, cramming the tape into the machine and adding, "It's a sing-along."

Well, kumbai-fucking-yah.

After she sets up their evening entertainment, she tosses down three nips this time. As John does every night of late, he offers one to each of his co-captives, only to be summarily rejected. He likes that this is her gift just for him. And it's nightly. Not just a one-time favorite meal or a one-time favorite song. He leans onto the heel of one palm and pulls back a sip, pacing himself as he's learned to do, though the heavy stew will soak the liquor up nicely. Maybe that's why she gave him three tonight.

And, of course, a slow song comes on. A love song. Eric Clapton at his best. Enchanted by the sweet tones of "Wonderful Tonight," John watches her sing. It's demure, and *H* sings along almost right away. She sounds better than he does, but she's also had steady water intake for her entire life. Both of them look lost in the music, and John wonders if this is a special song for them. He doesn't know how she lured *H* in, but both he and *A* were seduced. Hell, *A* said he was even in love with her once. Looking at the duet, John feels that dull sting of jealousy again. *A* just eats methodically, ignoring what's going on around them. Seems like both of his co-captives are good at ignoring each other's "moments." Meanwhile, John's not sure he could ever look away.

———

The radio is now a nightly thing. She's moved on to more recent pop music. It's the same five songs the radio stations play on repeat eight million times a day, but neither *H* nor *A* have heard any of them before. It's sweet. Refreshing. Fascinating. John didn't realize music had evolved, but *A* is marveling at how lyrics aren't even veiled innuendos anymore. *H* never asks to change the tune but only bops along when she switches to classic rock.

I knew he was a Guns N' Roses kind of guy. John smirks to himself.

He leans back on his cot and nurses his nightly nip. It's a sex on the beach drink mix, and he wonders if she's hinting at something. He's considered masturbating under his blanket while the others are asleep, but no real inspiration ever comes to him. When he thinks of his wife, it only makes him sad, and he never really bothered to remember faces otherwise. There's only Jane's now, except that makes him wither like a prune whenever it crosses his mind.

This is like camping, he supposes. He's fallen into his routine of eating, digging, and sleeping, and isn't that all the majority of humans want? Predictable contentment? Sadly, this is a healthier routine than he'd had before The Bitch had plucked him out of the real world and shoved him in a hole. Down here, he only has one vice, recently reintroduced into his life. It's liquid and numbing, and probably only exists to keep him docile, but at least he has a cute-ish dealer.

Once the thought crosses his mind, he frowns into his bottle.

She looks nothing like Beth. She looks normal. Average. A real-life plain Jane. The sort of person other people see and then immediately forget about. She blends. She still has a pretty mouth though. A pretty voice too. Pretty laugh. And a fair body shape, if he's being honest with himself. Enough hips to grab, even though the rest of her is fairly small.

His body stirs and it's absolutely unwanted. He needs to get out of here soon or he's going to start fucking himself up just for a chance to ride the unconscious Viagra tour.

She hits a high note for a half second before she botches it and croaks like a little frog. Everyone has a good laugh once she laughs at herself. She seems to be having fun these past few days. She's even letting some things slide that *A* and *H* absolutely panic over. John still doesn't know any better sometimes.

He regards this vicious/not-vicious woman, throwing his remorse and regret in her direction. If her man had only treated her right, so many things could have been different. Maybe some things still could. They say, if you truly love something, you'll let it go. Perhaps she just needs to learn to love them enough to set them free. Though John knows better. If anything, she'll hold on tighter.

Whatever his wife is doing now, at least she's not a temperamental, borderline psychotic mess. Or is she? Does Beth even know he's gone? Does anybody? John had long since lost all his friends, stopped contracting for gigs, and never really hit the same bars more than once. If anyone misses him, it's probably the people he paid on a regular basis. His landlord, who's probably pretty pissed right about now. His pharmacist, who may or may not be annoyed that he's not picking up his 'scripts. Oddly enough, his therapist might be the only one who'd send the police banging down doors to find him, wondering if he'd just gone on a bender or finally offed himself.

No. If he wants out, it's on his own dime. John has no knight in shining armor to come save him. Looking at the two men who sing idiotically under the thrall of this average Helen of Troy, John realizes that *he* is the knight in shining armor. Now more than ever. They're getting too cozy. Too safe. Too docile.

Laughing, *A* sits on the cot beside him, smacking him on the healed-over letter on his chest with a grin. "You gonna join in the party or what?"

John just nods at Jane, lifting his little bottle and making her follow suit. She takes another glug of liquor, closing her eyes. and John whispers the word, *"Tonight."*

A looks at him with wide eyes before schooling his face back into feigned amusement. He nods a little before asking, "You gonna sing or what?"

John ticks his chin in her direction and calls out, "You got any PSY? I'm feeling some Korean 'Gangnam Style' right about now!"

The other men turn to him like he's breathed fire, but she just gives him a sly look with a hiccup. She's a little slurry, teetering on the edge of drunk, and is likely to sleep like a baby while he runs far, far away.

"Nuh-uh!" She puts her hand on her chin with wide eyes. "Lies! No way you can sing that!"

It's not a true sign of disbelief. It's a challenge.

Gauntlet thrown, his grin is stunning. "Try me."

THE PAST -
INTERLUDE ONE

He hates this. Ohhhhh, he hates this, he hates this, he hates this! His lips are numb and he can't breathe, panic threatening to settle in and get cozy directly in his chest. At home, this would be when his mom would bust out the brown paper bag and tell him to, "Slow it down, Johnny. Nice and even."

Staring at him, John's friend of the day is unsure of what to do. "Dude, calm down! It's gonna be alright. Why are you freaking out about something you're good at?"

John ignores him and thinks about his mom instead, steadying his breath and trying to find an even keel while picturing the brown paper bag inflating and deflating like a crinkling balloon.

In, out, in, out.

Now, let's be clear. John is absolutely *not* nervous about his public speaking class. It suits him. Anyone at school will tell you that all he does is run his mouth, regardless of who's listening or how much trouble it might get him into. So, no, John's tummy isn't in a twist over that. It's because *she* just transferred into class and is sitting in the first row. You know, the one right in front of where he's supposed to stand, wave his arms around, "own the moment," and charm his bored peers into submission.

John's friend catches his line of sight and hums as if pleased. "At least you have good taste."

"I've...wanted her...for years," John admits, still trying to slow his burning lungs.

"You and everyone else. Not gonna happen. She's frosty." His buddy pats his shoulder, willing him to settle down.

"Do you think...she's...a lesbian?" John asks, picturing all sorts of wonderful things in his mind.

"Nah. Hot, but nah. She just hates us."

"Us?"

"You know. Us assholes." He lifts his finger and twirls it wide, whether indicating the world at large, men at large, or just present company is up for interpretation.

John snorts, regaining his equilibrium and his breath, pins and needles fading into normality. "Speak for yourself... I'm the perfect gentleman."

"Tell that to your fifteen girlfriends."

John scoffs, tired now, though he'll never admit it. Stupid panic attacks. "It's not like that." Not that he's proud of it. "They just wanna hang out with me 'cause I've got charisma."

"Yeah, I'll bet." His friend rolls his eyes. "Then why don't you get out there and charisma her off her feet."

Maybe he could. Girls do like him. John's good looking. Smart. Funny too, but in an "Ohmigawd, I can't believe you just said that!" kind of way. He's a senior who's blazing a hot trail toward Salutatorian because Valedictorians are too expensive. Living in this hick town with his penniless parents, John will be lucky if he can afford a community college, never mind a brand name one, and that's even if he comes to the plate with a few scholarships in his pocket. He's not going to let that slow his roll though. He's going to make something of himself. He's gotta aim high, otherwise he'll never be able to afford the twenty-one-some-odd kids he wants to have.

Brash and raring to go, ready to prove his excellence to the world and to the girl of his dreams, John stomps out to the front of the room with undeniable confidence!

...And immediately trips over the pretty girl's sneakered feet.

She yelps and he twists, landing on his ass with a harsh bark, immediately backing up on his heels and wanting, hard-core, to die. He sputters, "Why'd you do that?" over and over until his mouth almost falls off.

"I didn't mean it!" she squeals.

He returns her petulant tone. "I didn't say you meant it! I only said, 'Why?'"

"It was an accident! I was just stretching!"

Asshole friend chimes in. "A likely story."

Both John and what is now the love of his life whirl on the boy and yell, "Shut up!"

Asshole puts both hands in the air, surrendering immediately with a ridiculous smirk as the teacher walks in. Mr. Durn is an on-again, off-again actor who tries to make ends meet by teaching teenagers not to piss themselves in front of a large crowd. An admirable skill. He cocks his head at John as he lays prostrated in front of the student body, wincing over the new crack in his ass.

"Well, Jonathan, I suppose that's one way to warm up before a presentation."

Asshole mouths, *"Jonathan?"* and John just shakes his head. Mr. Durn embellishes by default. Brads become *Bradleys* and Christys become *Christinas.* That's why John's not surprised when the teacher calls out the incorrectly extended name, "Bethany, why don't you help the boy up, since you're the reason he'll be visiting the proctologist later today."

The class chuckles, and the attention makes her cheeks burn, humiliated and turning redder than her curlicue hair. It's swept back in a messy bun with just the right amount of tendrils framing her face. She takes it down and puts it back up again in irritation, a nervous habit John's seen from afar and finds adorable.

For his part, John stays exactly where he is, waiting for their inevitable connection to spark when she helps him stand. Their fingers will touch. Their lips will part. They'll look at each other, lost in time for a moment, unable to stop destiny from uniting them as one. John even considers feigning a broken ankle to get her to escort him to the nurse's office. He'll lean on her ever so slightly, smelling the scent of her hair. That's when she'll look at him, so remorseful for causing his pain, and let her lips graze his cheek in apology. He lives a life-time in a millisecond, letting it all begin and end with her.

Huffing, she mutters and rears back violently, scraping the whole desk across the floor, never mind just the chair. When she advances on him, *feisty* is written all over every inch of her perfect, freckled face. John would freak out about the raw potential of this moment, but there is no pause before one slender hand wrenches the back of his collar, choking him, while the other one slips under his armpit, dragging him up as if he wasn't a good fifty pounds heavier than her.

He's in love. Goddamnit, he's in love. And he's never washing that armpit again.

Meanwhile, she's growling something unintelligible he barely hears. Thrusting him center-stage in a whirlwind, she sits back down, her mouth pulling so deeply into a frown that it's more like a scowl as her stare burns holes in her fidgeting hands, refusing to look up.

John is speechless. Which sucks because he's supposed to give a speech.

The teacher gestures for him to begin as if his heart isn't

on fire. He stands in front of the class, hair mussed and holding himself like a monkey, shoulders forward, arms loose, and mouth agape.

When she finally connects her gaze to his glassy stare, he blurts, "I'm in love with you. Will you go out with me?"

And the fury on her face gives him immediate regrets.

———

He doesn't expect it when her locker door opens ricochet fast, hitting him in the face with a loud *bang*. He does, however, expect her following grunt of amusement and half-hearted mutter of, "Oops."

John holds his nose, his eyes watering from the impact. "Look, I'm sorry, okay? I didn't mean to embarrass you."

She doesn't dignify it with a response, slamming her locker closed and turning on her heels instead. John, completely aware that he's an idiot, follows her at close range.

"Okay, okay, okay, you don't have to go out with me—"

"You don't say," she mutters.

"—but maybe we can start as friends or something." John ducks in front of her, holding his arms out in a placating gesture. Her cheeks are on fire with a fierce blush, nearly hiding her freckles. Twisting her upper body, she dodges him with books in hand, but catches his elbow by mistake, sending them all to the speckled linoleum floor with a fluttering series of plops. The sound she makes is volcanic, made worse by the fact that John dives down to help her, putting their faces all too close. That's when she shoves him on his ass again.

He winces out a hiss, tailbone definitely bruised. "I'll take that as a 'no' vote on friendship," he groans, lying flat on the floor and just letting his backside hate him.

"What is wrong with you?" she asks through her teeth.

Taking a beat to feel the cool flooring under his shoulder blades, John shrugs with his eyes closed. The other students mill around him, somehow managing to not step on his head.

"Ever seen *Wayne's World*?" John asks.

"What does that have to do with—?"

He cuts her off, quoting, "'She will be mine. Oh, yes, she will be mine.' That's the only thing I think of whenever I look at you."

It's only then that he dares peek at her. Beth is gobsmacked. He seals his eyes shut again in short order.

"I repeat, what is *wrong* with you? That's the creepiest thing I've ever heard!"

"Or!" He holds up a finger. "Maybe it's the most romantic." He lets his hand flop back down with a little *thump*.

She glowers at him. "You've never even spoken to me before! What is it you think I'm going to do? Swoon? Cheerlead? Do a split? People like you think they can have whatever they want, don't they? Girls fawn all over you because they believe you'll be their ticket out of here, so what now? You're just gonna assume when you tell me to jump, I'm gonna say, 'How high?'"

He looks at her, eyes wide. "Nobody *fawns!*"

"Well, you listen to me. I'm not someone who will just roll over, beg for scraps, and bark like a dog for you!"

"Of course not. You'll only growl." He grins.

She proves him right, but it does him no favors. "People like you are assured a future beyond this hellhole just because you're self-important, cocky, and arrogant!"

"And smart."

"Meanwhile, people like me are just expected to make babies, get old, and die here. But I'm going to prove everyone wrong. That's not in the cards for me. I'll go to New York or L.A. or Japan! And I'm going to get there on my own merit.

I'm not going to lower myself to getting married to some enti-tled prick like you just to ride your coattails out of here!"

"Whoa. Wait. Slow down. Who said you'd be riding my coattails anywhere? Though it's nice of you to assume we're getting married."

Beautiful Beth puts her hands in her hair and tugs at her ponytail again with the deepest *"Uuuugh!"* John's ever heard.

He interrupts her conniption with, "I hear you're good at math."

She looks up at him as if she has the urge to kill. "What?"

"You're also in AP English. You're into dance and theater, but you would rather paint the sets than be on stage. If I go by the art class' portfolio showcase, you seem to like charcoal the best, and you draw like someone from the Renaissance."

Her urge to kill is fading, it seems. Instead, she looks... unmoored. Her voice takes on a whispery tone. "Again, that's creepy."

He sits up on his elbows and repeats, "Or maybe it's romantic."

There is a pause as he looks at the floor, collecting his words.

"I meant what I said in class, even though I said it in the stupidest of ways. I hear people talk about you and my ears zero in on it. I see you in the hall and I can't look anywhere else. You seem so driven, and I wish I knew what goal you're aiming for. I want to know what you're thinking about. What makes you tick.

"I don't assume I'll get anything I want. I'm just the kind of guy who tries hard and doesn't stop. But I'm not like you. I can't really see the end game. I don't know what I want to be, except that I want to be good at it when I get there." He looks at her again, earnest and probably too serious for an on-the-floor-in-the-hallway conversation. "But you seem to be running down a specific path. Like everything you do is intentional. If you say you want to get out of here, then you're going to get out of here. If there's anyone's coattails to ride on here, it's yours."

Her mouth opens...and closes. Once. Twice. Speechless.

How he'd love to pepper kisses on her lips. The dappling of red stars over the bridge of her nose and cheeks. Her eyelids. His heart aches while she struggles to respond.

And the damn bell for next period rings.

They blink at each other, completely oblivious to the crowd fanning around them and staring with little smirks. They're just two kids unsure of what to do next.

Finally, she clears her throat. "I guess you know my name, since you're a stalker."

His lips turn up at the corners as he nods. "It's Beth." Her face somehow burns brighter, now reaching the tips of her ears and her collarbone. He takes it as an absolute compliment. "Do you know mine?"

"It's Idiot," she states, looking away. "Absolute Total Idiot. Junior."

He has a full-blown grin now. "I'll take it."

He rushes to help her gather her books and tries not to fumble while she keeps tossing soft insults at him.

"Moron. Stalker. Inappropriate. Creepy."

He brushes her hand by accident, so cliché and also so awesome. When she looks at him, she freezes up, so he fills the space between them with words.

"I'm also nice," he says.

"Maybe nice," she agrees.

"And funny."

"If by funny, you mean weird."

"And cute."

At that, she scoffs.

"But not as cute as you," he adds softly.

Sputtering, she hikes her books up higher, holding them

to her chest like a security blanket. Second bell's about to ring, so he better scoot. He's already going to be late as it is.

"I'm very pleased to meet you, Beth. Officially."

She nods, out of her depth. "Yeah. Okay."

"And I'm excited to get to know you," he says, pressing his luck.

She rolls her eyes, but finally cracks a smile.

"And I'm more than happy to ride your coattails when you marry me."

This time, she grins, even though she's not looking at him. Chewing her lower lip, she says, "Maybe before that, we should just be friends."

"I'd like that. I'll even let you call me Idiot."

She giggles, and it twines the thread of destiny around his heart. He has half a mind to throw himself on her and...what? Hug her and kiss her and cry a little bit?

Before he has a chance, she walks away, which is probably for the best.

Second bell rings, but he's two floors away from his class. A stern look, a talking-to, a detention—who knows what's coming his way. It doesn't matter though. If he gets in trouble for the sake of this moment, maybe that's kind of romantic too.

Home Sweet Home

“This is not helping!” John growls at *H*, who sits on his bed with his head curled to his knees. Already filthy, he rinses the laundry basket down the altar grate, washing away any dirt in case he can't get them out tonight. He has no idea how high up he is or if he can break through the surface, but he's working like a man possessed and has the scrapes all over his elbows, belly, and knees to prove it. He's returned to his bare-skinned-self, not wanting to dirty his clothes, but he's more than given up caring about his nudity at this point.

“I'm just saying we don't know what's out there,” *H* says.

“*So?*” John hisses, hating the delay of launching himself back and up into the fray.

H's eyes are wide, his fingers clamping together in prayer. John can swear he sees the beat of the man's heart through his all too visible rib cage. “What if there's a huge fence to climb with barbed wire or something? Acres of land? Forests and wolves and bears?”

“Oh-fucking-my! I guess we'll have to brave that if we come to it, won't we?” John grits his teeth as he gestures upward. "All I know is the dog is prowling around. If it takes out rabbits, it would definitely catch us. I don't know about you, but I have no desire to be mauled. We need to try and be quiet and sneak away to *wherever* without getting its attention. You heard the truck when it went back and forth. The house or barn or whatever is not far."

H starts rocking. "Why are we doing this?"

"I thought you didn't want to die here!"

"I don't want to die, period!" *H* says, throwing daggers with his glare.

A stands straight as a board, not looking at either of them, just staring up at the stars and planets that glitter in the black. "You wanna know something?"

No, I want to dig, John thinks, every part of him tense and ready to throttle these men.

Head tilted skyward, *A* says, "She had two other guys up there with me."

John stills immediately and *H*'s head snaps up quick.

A, for his part, looks as if he's lost behind his own eyes. "You think we look bad? *They* looked bad. Always asleep. Tubes down their throats and between their legs. What she did to me up there, she couldn't do to them. Not anymore. They were too used up. God knows how long they've been like that." *A* looks at *H*—not sad, not mean, just honest. "Would you rather be dead, or them? Because eventually we'll end up there. Kept alive in a different kind of Fishbowl. One made of beds and bedsores." *A* muses, "How many did she take that never ended up down here? How many more does she have in that house that I didn't see?"

Horrified, John asks, "Why didn't you say anything before?"

A regards him with an indefinable expression. "There are a lot of things I don't say."

John stares at their circle of sky, deciding then and there

that there is nothing they can do for those other men. There's no way to control her reaction when she wakes up to find her favorite trio of pets gone either. "Don't get any ideas," he says. "The only ones we're saving right now are ourselves. The best thing we can do for anyone else is get up and get out. Run for help."

"Yeah," *H* says bitterly. "And who in their right mind is going to help the stranger knocking on their door in the middle of the night with his dick hanging out? They're more likely to shoot it off than anything else."

"Well, thank Christ for our man-jammies then." John is so done with this conversation. He stalks up to *H* with fire in his eyes. "You told me you needed to get out. That you were with us on this. If you've changed your mind, then stay. I wonder what she'll think when she finds out you've been keeping a secret from her all this time. Especially one this big."

At that, the other man's eyes blow wide, his pupils narrowing like pinpricks. John lets that sentiment run through *H*'s mind like the hard fact it is.

"Dig or die. Now, I'd appreciate any help you can give, but if you're tapped out, the least you can do is shut up."

Silently, *A* takes the laundry basket from John's arms while *H* folds into himself, his face twisted in a never-ending grimace.

Fine.

John's going to take him out kicking if he has to...though screaming is out of the question.

John's past the point of claustrophobia when his finger pokes through the roots of the grass into the free air above.

The cool breeze feels so alien that he yanks back, causing a tiny hole to shine starlight down on him like a holy revelation. There is no moon, but his eyes are so used to the dark John can clearly see blades of grass, almost blue under the night's shade.

He needs to widen this tunnel area before he can breach the surface any further, but his heart is in this throat with hope. In the thick of it, John rakes his hands along his body to push the soil down his sides and between his legs while *A* collects solemnly below. This is like being buried alive, but John keeps his eyes on the prize. A cool bit of air ruffles the stalks of grass that surround his single ray of hope. Hopefully it will be the last dark frame that will ever restrict John's view of the world.

Slithering out of his burrow, he tips his chin up in triumph, looking at *A* with all the pride in the universe. "So, what are you gonna do when we get out of here?"

The man blinks at him, looking at the tunnel as understanding dawns on his face, knowing that they've broken through. "I'm gonna hoard food and get fat. Really fat. Like, 'I need a wheelchair to go anywhere' fat."

John nods with a smirk and looks at *H*. "You?"

He stares at John with shimmering eyes, clutching his blanket and wringing it endlessly. "Even if I get out, I'm going to spend my whole life feeling like I'm down here. No matter where I am or who I'm with, I'm always going to be right here."

John and *A* connect gazes. What is there to say to that?

Instead, John tries to continue his pep talk of optimism. "I'm going to get my wife back. I made her fall in love with me once, I can do it again. All I need is time. After this, she'll listen to me. If I know her, even if she hates me, she'll take care of me. That's when I'll get my chance." He believes that with his whole heart. "I'll make it right. We're gonna be happy again."

He looks at his uprooted stones laying on the Fishbowl floor, the inanimate objects forever unaware of what saviors they are. John runs his eyes over the uneven surface of the well for the last time. With a smile that looks on the verge of manic, he says, "The time cometh nigh and all that jazz. Give me a bit longer to widen this for you guys and then I want you right behind me in that tunnel. We need to get up and out quick. I'm not going to tear through until all of us are ready."

Both other men nod in understanding.

John waves his hand at the hose. "We need that metal thing." He splits his fingers in the tell-tale peace sign. "The spike will help if we need to lever open any windows or locks. Yeah?"

H nods. "I'll take it."

Good. Give the guy something to be responsible for.

Pointing at *H,* John says, "You come up next then. You're still the weakest," he nods in *A*'s direction, "so you need to shove if it comes down to it, and I'll pull from the top. Make sense?"

He yanks on his pajamas again before diving back into his work. Indeed, any rescuers would probably be put off by a naked man flailing and screaming for help. Though it might be better if they can't see his cartoonish clothes in the dark. They might question his sanity.

———

His friends are crammed in behind him, shoved so far up his ass that John is glad to have his pjs on. *H*'s cheek is basically riding his anus at this point, and *A* is shoving upward from the bottom of the tunnel. The added benefit is that this way there's little chance of *H* backing out before they get him under the canopy of the sky. At that point, they can only pray that hope rears its pretty head and kicks him into gear.

John can feel the flimsiness of the loam above him. It sags over his shoulders as he peeks out of his already-collapsing poke hole. Ready to tear himself out of the grass like the proverbial *Night of the Living Dead*, John trembles, but there's no way in hell he's turning back now. Everything in him is screaming to panic, but he won't. He won't, he won't, he *can't*. If he does, this will all be over before it begins.

"Ready?" he whispers.

"No," both men reply in tandem.

He scoffs at them. "Jinx."

Muffled from the bottom, *A* adds, "But that doesn't mean we're not doing it anyway."

John shakes his head back and forth with a perfunctory "*pfft*," trying to get a little crumble off his face before it ends up in his eyes. Hyper aware, the smells and sounds become cacophonous, pounding into every nerve of his body. It's silent except for the soothing ambience of breezes and crickets, but it does nothing to calm him. John's afraid to stop now, but can't help pausing to take a breath. How long has it been since he felt fresh air?

Enthralled, he reaches, slowly tearing a large swath up, his arm rending the clinging roots of the grass.

And hears the jingle all too late.

The meat of John's hand is clamped on, the dog snarling and whipping its head back and forth, teeth tearing into John's flesh. It rips and splits open as Cujo tugs backward in jarring lurches that light John up with pain.

He can't scream. He can't let himself scream. But he can't pull away either. The men below him are shoving him out from behind, up and into the maw of the monster.

Not a Rottweiler. Not a shepherd. Thin, just like she said, but strong as a motherfucker as it pulls John forward. His eyes run with tears, and he lets out low, muffled whines and grunts.

A gets up from the rear and automatically goes for broke, though the dog already has what it needs, refusing to follow. John's arm thrashes back and forth as the dog tries to shred his palm to pieces, the flesh now a ruddy red that he can't look away from.

He's a rabbit. He's a fucking rabbit that had dug out of a fucking burrow and now his hand is on fire.

Don't scream, don't scream, John begs himself, whimpering but unable to stop. Every time he scrambles forward on his hands and knees to relieve the pressure, the dog rears away and clenches its jaw, digging in as John comes closer and closer to revealing them all with a hollow cry.

He can't see through the pain anymore, eyes cinched closed and his whole body dragging over the dew. He needs to go cold. He needs to numb out to get through this. But he can't. Oh God, he can't.

There is a rough *chonk* sound, and the dog's grip goes slack. He peers up and *H* looms above, straddling the thing, the prong embedded in its eye. It's angled backward and spiking through the thing's brain, a steep, arced thrust from behind doing the perfect job. Cujo didn't even have time to yelp.

It would be perfect if not for John's hand.

H opens the thing's teeth and what John pulls out is a mess of blood and fingers sticking up at the wrong angles. It burns, it burns, and he's going to pass out. Face spattered, *H* grabs John's cheeks, lifting his head and mouthing the word, *"Breathe."*

So that's what John does. Getting up to his haunches, he tucks his mangled hand under his opposite armpit, no other idea of what else to do with the throbbing mess. His lips are trembling, but *H* helps him up, holding his face once more.

He whispers, *"Breathe, John."*

And it's the first time he's ever said his name.

John stifles a sob and nods.

In a choice between fight or flight, John chooses fight and looks around him. *A* is forty feet away, standing in the shadow of a farmhouse, assessing doors and windows. Indeed, there are high fences with razor wire and pastures in the distance where cows stand, asleep. White, stocky bodies with black spots, just barely visible in the acres surrounding them. Even if the three of them can get off property, how far until they find someone else? What direction do they even go in?

One thing at a time, the voice of his mother rings in his head. *Breathe in and out, Johnny boy. In and out.*

So that's what he does, putting painful pressure on his raging hand and stumbling toward the man in the distance.

Don't scream. Don't scream.

A has looked over the barn. Turning over his shoulder and gesturing at the door, he hooks his pointer fingers together to signify a lock. He goes to the first-floor windows next, delicately pressing them up with no luck.

There are six windows on the first level and a screened-in porch that's sure to creak. *H* is clutching at his own shoulders, his arms crossed against his chest as he reviews everything with wide, panicked eyes. Joining their friend close to the hose that runs to the Fishbowl, John sees *H* nod at a metallic monstrosity humming at the side of the house.

"Walk-in freezer," he whisper-mouths at them. *"We need to get in there."*

"What good will that do?" *A* asks.

"It goes straight through. You can access it from two doors— inside, outside—unless something's changed."

Both men look at *H* in confusion. Slightly dazed, *H*'s

mouth is a flat line. Pale with shock, he stammers, *"This is my house."*

———

There are no lights on in the freezer. It's borderline arctic and John's lightly slippered feet immediately ache as they rest on the uneven, crunchy piles of frost gathered on the floor. He can't see, it's too dark, but he knows his breath is making pretty clouds in the frigid air. The goosebumps are immediate under the thin fabric of his clothes, but he can't rub his arms to warm himself or he'll shriek with pain. The numbness of shock is setting in, which is a good thing, though John knows it will also lower his body temperature, and that can only be bad. Plusses and minuses. Until John goes full-blown la-la land though, his hand is one huge scream, and he's not sure he'll ever be able to use it again.

There is a window-shaped haze of light diagonally across from the entrance, but it's not enough to make anything visible, especially when the outer door shuts behind them, leaving them in the black.

There's a *slap* sound and *A* makes a little grunt. Looking toward the noise, John also slams into something, smashing his nose. It's cold and freezes to his skin almost instantly.

Pounding, John's mind growls the word: *Meat locker.*

He staggers away, disoriented as he slaps off another slab.

H finds a light switch on the wall, and fluorescents blink on in a flicker. John cringes, hiding his eyes under his good wrist and tweaking his bad hand in the process, making him bite back a deep moan as he begins to sweat. A very bad thing to do in a place like this.

When the spots behind his eyelids recede, all John sees is

the blood on the ground, frozen in pink crystals. Drag marks and scuff marks and handprints.

Handprints.

John's head rears up.

Bodies in different stages of butchering hang from hooks on the ceiling. Three humans, skinned and trimmed. Muscles and sinew. White tendons and frosty pink slabs stretched between them. The figures look like upside down anatomy drawings, but the faces...the faces are untouched in all their horrific splendor.

John's mind screams something new.

THE MEAT! THE SALTED MEAT!

And he knows, without a shadow of a doubt, that all this time...he's been eating them.

A's stomach lets go and *H*'s eyes are round circles. None of them says a word. Not a damn word. Watching the men they'd bumped into swing gently back and forth on their frozen hooks, the escapees back out of the inner door into the unnatural warmth of a kitchen.

It looks like something out of *Better Homes and Gardens*, all warm tones and special hand towels sporting chickens, pigs, cows, and all kinds of farm-things in burgundy reds and ochre yellows.

T'was the night before Christmas...

There are skylights in the ceiling, another geometric frame around an open sky, but there are three of them this time, making it seem more inviting even while their surfaces are hazed with the pollution of rain and pollen.

...and all through the house...

There is nothing on the countertops. No teapots, no toasters. No knife blocks. Just the smooth, reflective surface of pretty marble. A surgeon's salary gives you access to all the finer things, it seems.

...not a creature could stir when locked up like a mouse.

The refrigerator's outer door matches the cabinetry. Everything is a creamy sort of beige with beveled edges, and John just knows the drawers must have that soft-close functionality. The one that makes it so you can't slam something by accident —or even on purpose. Oddly enough, they all have child locks on them. Too bad John's hands don't both work or he'd go digging for buried treasure. *A* is about to do it for them when *H* places a soft hand on his forearm and shakes his head.

He mouths, *"Quiet."*

He's not wrong. Rifling around in drawers is bound to wake up Sleeping Beauty, no matter how tipsy she might have been at lights out.

"It's almost over," John whispers, his voice catching on itself.

"Just leave and live," *A* agrees.

This was never about revenge. This is, and always has been, a plan of escape. No one needs to be searching loudly for carving knives, and the prong is lost somewhere deep inside Cujo's skull.

Good.

John edges in front of the others, tip-toeing his way across the wooden floor to the doorframe. The color of it matches the rest of the wood grain that climbs the walls, making this another unnervingly monochrome space to play in. John wants nothing more than technicolor.

...Skinned men were all hung by Plain Jane without care, visions of pain found behind their blind stare.

With A *in Tweety bird, and* H *fixed to snap, John's moments away from his brain going crack.*

One floorboard creak will ruin everything. Placing his steps ever-so-lightly, John peers out of the kitchen door at an angle, letting it shield him. Beyond, he sees a dark living room, only lit by the kitchen's ambience. *A* creeps up from behind as they assess the situation, trying to find the exit to the outside, looking past the fluffy sectional couches and the stacked book-shelves. They find it at the end of the hall, as far to the right as they can possibly get. Above the door is a picture of *H* in the tell-tale tuxedo of his wedding photo. Young. Healthy. Perfect hair and perfect smile, arms wrapped around his soon-to-be scorned bride as she stares at him with unending love in her eyes. Pigtails. A sweet mouth.

The Bitch.

John's mouth drops wide.

Fuck...

John hears a gasp, suddenly aware of his own shadow casting a shape on the carpet ahead of him, and pulls back against the wall, knowing in his heart that it's already too late.

The gun fires just as his head clears the entryway, the wood blasting from the door frame as buckshot pummels through it, tearing splinter-stripes on John's cheeks. When he dares glance back, The Bitch is standing, reloading a shotgun with an iconic *snap-snap!*

A sees it too, and throws himself off John, directly into the line of fire. Before John can blink, *A* pivots around *H*, and thrusts him at the woman just as the next shot rings out, blowing the back of *H*'s head out, and he falls in a heavy clump.

The screech she lets out is like carpenter nails lifting up flaps of John's skin.

A grabs John fast and ducks around her as she rushes forward. It's only moments before he hears her scream, *"JOHN!"* and instinct makes him turn in her direction, trip-ping over himself and landing on his knees.

But she's not looking at him.

She's curled around *H* and wailing, cradling him and scream-whimpering John's name over and over. Something in him cries out, *I'm sorry. I didn't mean it! I didn't want that to happen!* but *A* yanks him up into a stumble, throwing him farther into the house and toward the door. She's keening as *A* throws the deadbolts, but there's one lock that's key-only. He scrabbles at it, but her bellow lets them know they're out of time.

...When out in the kitchen there arose such a clatter, I begged, "Pretty please, don't serve me on a platter."

A latches onto John's bad hand and he howls as it tweaks. Something else in his mangled palm lets go with a broken snap.

Breathless, *A* launches them into the first open door that exists and shoves him inside.

"Why is she calling my name?" John weeps, hearing her unending wails for him. What does she want? Does she blame him? Because she should. Is he going to go in the freezer?

A shoves at a dresser, angling his shoulder for leverage and getting the furniture to scrape its way in front of the door. "She's not calling for you," he grinds out, the effort taking everything he's got. With a meaningful look, he says, "We're all named John."

Barricade barely in place, *A* looks around in a blur, seeing a window that he already knows won't open. Lashing out, he snatches a sturdy bedside lamp and holds it tight.

And that's when the shotgun blasts through the door at head level, trying to get at anyone she can as she releases both barrels.

A doesn't let that distract him as he pummels the glass window. It shatters while John stares at the holes in the wood, mind flashing to the holes in *H*'s head. *A* grabs a pillow and rolls out the open glass, screaming for John to do the same, but he is frozen. His eyes are opened wide and his breath is coming too fast again, the numbness and the black spots and the faintness falling on him as his lungs balloon.

The *CLACK-CLACK* comes all too fast and the door bursts open, the dresser flinging to the side like the lightweight, empty thing it likely is. The muzzle of the gun thrusts through the gap in a straight line as he stares.

With another *BLAM,* the escaping *A* is no more, and she swivels as soon as she catches John in her peripheral vision.

He stares down the shotgun's double-barrel black holes with its deadly sight aimed right at his face. He can't breathe. He can't breathe and he's dying and he's already dead and he's meat in the freezer.

Her mouth is a sneer as John manages five words.

"You m-make me eat them…"

And he passes out.

THE PAST - Prelude

John is fourteen and his grandparents are impressed when he shoves the sushi in his mouth, cold and salted with soy sauce. They're even *more* impressed when he lays on a thin layer of wasabi, praying to the Gods that this won't suck as much as his mom said it would. John will eat anything and everything because—

"...Johnny boy, you've got to eat," his mom begs. "The doctor says you don't have enough in you and you're getting sick. I need you to eat!"
"But, Mom," the ten-year-old whines.
"No buts! You're gonna die, Johnny. Is that what you want? Do you want to die? Because—"

Fruits and veggies are the best. But no meat! Johnny hates meat. It feels weird in his mouth. Smooshy and wrong. It makes him gag. It comes from animals, and Johnny doesn't want to eat the animals. He doesn't want the cheese or the milk or the anything! He went to the farm once and the animals were all so sad. Johnny wants them to be free because

Johnny is five and he is free, and everything deserves to be free. Besides, cows like carrots too, just like Johnny likes carrots, and—

Orange good! Yellow good! Green best!
Mama makes an airplane and it fliiiiiies into his
mouth. He loves it when the airplane goes around
with a *pbbbbbbthhhhh*!!!

He giggles, cold moosh on his chinny-chin-chin.
"Mama!"
John-john makes the hand sign for "More." He knows
more and *sleep* and *ouch*. Mama says he needs more
words, but until then, he has chubby-wubby hands.

Pbbbbbbbbtthhhhhhhh!!

"Mama! Mama! Mama!" John-john opens his mouth
and laughs and laughs.
Because love.
Because good.
Because "Mama!"

NOW

"Mama..." John says out loud.

It's barely a sound at all. Soft but echoing endlessly. He's disoriented and his throat hurts. His everything hurts. He's weak and his muscles tremble when he tries to move. His bad hand twinges and aches, though not as much as it should. John's heavy eyes open slowly, and he blinks at it. It's covered in purple pockmarks and the fingers are still bent wrong, but these aren't fresh scabs. These are healed over. Scars. Still, it aches, but John is too tired to put any puzzle pieces together just now. He feels numb, like that stint he had making friends with Percocet.

He's in his bed. His cot.

But the other two are missing.

John's eyes blink too slowly as he rolls them around in a slow circle. The familiar bubble of sky looks down on him, sun casting a warm beam down onto the altar. But it looks strange. There are no...

Stones? Is that the word?

Instead, there is a rough sort of white.

Concrete.

Looking at the walls with fresh eyes, it seems that the Fishbowl has gotten some work done. Instead of a well, it's a cemented tomb. How The Bitch did it is anyone's guess. Perhaps there were some new, fresh men that she put out of their misery once the job was done.

I'm going to die here.

The thought comes and goes, passing over John's foggy mind as he almost falls into unconsciousness again, but a flex of his bad hand jolts him with just enough pain to bring him back to the moment. He feels gone inside. All gone. Forever gone.

Throat raw, he sits up like he's swimming in Jello. It's then that he sees the wicker food-basket, and his stomach churns. It can't be trusted. Whatever is in there, he doesn't want it...until a rumble tells him that, yes, he absolutely does.

The food basket is done up in pretty bows, like a present. It's just a few feet away from the bed on the little, upended laundry basket. Why he's been gifted with that makeshift table again makes no sense. There's no use for it. He has no clothes, naked once more. He has a cot, but no blankets, no pillows...

I've lost my privileges.

He looks at his body and finally starts seeing reality.

He's thin. Very, very thin. When they'd climbed up the hole, he wasn't like this. How long has he been asleep for? How long has he been *unconscious* for?

He stands and falls again immediately, scraping his skin on the rough texture of the mortar he's trapped in. Working his way over as gently and slowly as he can, he sees the contents of his gift basket. Vitamins. Utensils and plates. Ripped up paperback books, all romance novels. A set of familiar nips. And a small, plain white envelope with a lipstick kiss mark.

Hands trembling, John winces as he works to pick it up and take out the little card inside. The handwriting is girlish. It reads...

Dear John,
It's going to be okay.
You're the only one for me now.

Laughter bubbles up inside him. Slowly but surely, it comes harder and faster. Rough and harsh. Psychotic and maniacal. He doesn't bother feeling the pain in his heart as the giggles peel out of him, reverberating in this empty, and now concrete, coffin.

When the laughter subsides, the sobs come. Despair flows into him like black water, filling all his nooks and crannies. John rocks himself back and forth, back and forth. "You bitch. You fucking bitch. I'll kill you. I swear to God, I'll kill you."

His monologue is punctuated by a sickening thud, and his whole body freezes.

Slowly turning his head, John sees a crooked and broken human figure in a delicate sunbeam. It presents its newly broken edges to the light that cascades down from the Fishbowl's viewing platform. Caught in the rays is another blinding white paper tag wrapped around a crooked fingertip, so close, John can read it from here.

It says, simply, *For you,* with a crudely drawn fork and knife.

John fights back the bile rising in his throat but is unable. Doubling over, he dry-heaves wispy strands of wet silk into a clamped fist. Fire burning in his eyes, he slowly lifts his head to peer at the misshapen figure bleeding out on the ground.

"I'm not going to do it," he whispers fiercely. "I'm not going to eat you, John."

But even then, he's not so sure.

Author's Notes

This novella has come through many forms in its draft stage. Since I used to write for comic books (and still love that medium with a fierce passion), *Dear John* was originally a script for a dark, gritty, indie graphic novel. I went down the rabbit hole about it too. I've drawn sketches of the characters, panel layouts for scenes, schematics of the interior of the Fishbowl, an aboveground aerial shot of the house—all kinds of stuff—but let's face it. If this story had gone down the aisle that way, we would have ended up with significantly less nudity and dick jokes, which would be a true loss to the fine art of literature. But life is long, so perhaps this might find its way to the illustrated page yet. In the meantime, I'm so grateful that I was able to commission the talents of Yelenhol to bring these characters to life in fine lines. Their art is gritty and graceful, and I greatly enjoyed watching these doomed gentlemen come to life at the tip of their pen.

In the middle of its life, *Dear John* tried to be a novel. A nice, whopping, bull mastiff of pages. The problem was that it was a lot of filler. As fun as it was for me to think of stuff for our trio to do in their ample spare time, it wasn't much fun to read about, so I pulled a Jane and killed most of it, starving the rest. What's left is the best of what this story had to offer, and it's not over yet. John still has some escaping to do, and Jane needs to set up a new bag of tricks now that there is only one man in her life.

I know what will happen. But do you?

COMING IN JANUARY 2025
DEAR JANE

Jane wants a family,
and John has no choice.

About the Author

From the Boston suburbs, Nicholas Ferrante graduated with a BFA in animation and illustration from Lesley University / The Art Institute of Boston. Life consists of Hubsters, Spawn, writing, drawing, Star Wars, hot tea, and Saturday special breakfasts, which are the epitome of happiness.

There may also be a sudden influx of K-dramas on Netflix. The algorithm has dug deep under the skin.

Find more work in additional genres at nixcomix.com